danger city 2

URBAN SHORT FICTION

contemporary press

This is a work of fiction. All of the characters and events portrayed in this book are either products of the authors' twisted imaginations or are used fictitiously.

danger city 2

Photography and lettering by lilya
Cover design by Dennis Hayes, lilya and Chris Reese

A Contemporary Press Book
Published by Contemporary Press
Brooklyn, New York

Distributed by Publishers Group West
www.pgw.com

www.contemporarypress.com

ISBN 0-976657937

First Edition: November 2006

Printed in the United States of America

danger city 2

URBAN SHORT FICTION

RAW WORDS IN BROOKLYN

Over the years, we've thrown some great readings, some pretty good readings, and one or two that we cannot confirm ever actually occurred. Few, however, were as memorable as the unofficial debut of the collection you hold in your hands.

Late in August '06, we were offered a Thursday night at Bar 4, a great local bar in Brooklyn. In the lineup were CP cofounders and authors Jay Brida, Mike Segretto, Jess Dukes, and former intern/drug fiend/rock star Tony O'Neill.

The night went weird before it ever began. Tony arrived last, somewhat disturbed. On his way to the bar, someone started giving him trouble on 7th Avenue in Park Slope, a neighborhood known more for its million-dollar brownstones and more-organic-than-thou citizens than its crime. Tony pulled a knife, fully prepared to slice the guy six ways to Sunday. Thankfully, the gods of literature knew that Tony had a higher calling that evening, and the antagonist took the hint. Needless to say, Tony needed a drink to calm his nerves. We ordered him up a stiff one and prepared for show time.

The crowd began to pour in, although it was difficult to tell how many people were there for the reading and how many had come for the foosball table. For some still-puzzling reason, cover designer/Web site guru Dennis Hayes arrived dressed as a mime.

When everyone felt properly drunk and belligerent, it was time for the reading to begin. Tony went first, reading the CP classic "Balls," a story that has received a fantastic response in the past. Unfortunately, the foosball table had worked its foul magic on an extremely vocal section of the crowd. Even with the music off and the microphone cranked, Tony was fighting a losing battle. "Shut up!" he screamed at the foosballers, to no avail. "I'm going to cut off my own balls and eat them!" he insisted. Not even the promise of bloody, hilarious castration could distract the obsessed foosballers from their game. Tough crowd. Serious foosball. Tony rushed through the end of the story and left the stage, bruised, battered, and ready to drink the pain away.

Jay Brida was the next victim, reading his hardcore-lesbian-action-satire "Everyone's a Critic." Jay shouted until his throat was hoarse, but it did little to quell the ever-louder mob. It was clear that this was not going well. The only solution was to take an intermission and regroup, in the hopes that people were now so drunk they would forget we were ever there by the time the next readers were ready to go.

Renewed in drink and spirit, we forcefully reclaimed the stage. Mike Segretto got about one minute into "The Jersey Devil" when someone from the horde called, "take it off!" Like a savvy porn star, Mike knew that the only way to salvage his dignity would be to get naked. Off went the shirt, to deafening applause. And realizing that no one was still listening to his story, he pulled out the big guns: his 3rd and 4th nipples. The crowd went wild. Ever the professional, Segretto ended the reading bent-over in full moon.

Thankfully, by the time Jess Dukes kicked Segretto's socks off the stage and pulled up a stool, the crowd had whittled itself down to the people who actually wanted to be there for the reading. We ended the night with "Rita Carter," and left the audience pondering their masturbatory preferences.

The rest of the evening exists only as a hazy, half-remembered dream. Swept up in the festive mood, the bartenders decided to stop charging for drinks. Marriage vows were bent. Sexual orientations were questioned. More asses were bared. We vaguely remember taking a cab home, even though we live about two blocks away from the bar.

We may not be the most professional publishing house on the planet, but we do get to drink for free every now and again. Which, really, is about all one can ask for in this day and age. If you're ever in the New York area while we're having a reading, please drop by—everyone's welcome, even foosball fanatics.

In the meantime, enjoy these stories. We certainly do.

Contemporary Press

LINER NOTES

Balls by Tony O'Neill
"Balls" is dedicated to all of the writers who manage to defy the odds and hang onto theirs.

Bundy Is a God by Jon McCarron
Jon dedicates this, his second publication, to his sister-in-law Kristina since he was a forgetful ass and left her out of his liner notes the first time around. You're the best, Kris; a charming hell-cat with the soul of a saint that my brother was lucky enough to bring home to Mom.

Happy Happy Yumi-Chan by Jason William McNeil
With love always to Eden for showing me the joys of dangerous school girls!

First Draft by Craig McDonald
"First Draft" is dedicated to Svetlana Pironko and Michael O'Brien for believing, and to Charlie Stella for the nudge.

The Alcoholic Monkey by Jeffrey Dinsmore
Jeffrey Dinsmore (www.jeffreydinsmore.com) is the author of the CP novels *I, An Actress: The Autobiography of Karen Jamey* and *Johnny Astronaut* (as Rory Carmichael). He recently moved to Los Angeles to start the West Coast branch of Contemporary Press. He hasn't been heard from since.

The French Clock by Jeffrey Kuczmarski
Without the antics at the surreal school or the cheap booze-induced misadventures with Dusty, I may not have started or finished "The French Clock." Here's to old friends and getting that goddamn dead dog off the floor.

The Candy Man by Matthew Fries
For Grandma Turd.

Rita Carter by Jess Dukes
Some people can do pretty strange and fascinating things, if they try. This story is for them.

Everyone's a Critic by Jay Brida
Dedicated to George W. Bush, Dick Cheney, Dick Rumsfeld, and Condi Rice for making me believe the Four Horsemen of the Apocalypse actually exist.

Attack of the Deer by Carl Moore
I actually drew deer on some tights once. I'm not saying it was therapeutic, but it kept this from being a true story.

The Jersey Devil by Mike Segretto
Am I supposed to dedicate this story to someone here? Why would anyone want this filthy story dedicated to them? Nuts to that.

The Left Side by Ward Crockett
Ward Crockett would like to thank his lovely wife, his lovely family, and his lovely friends for their undying support and for turning a blind eye to certain unnamable crimes.

Teacher's Pets by Mike Cipra
Thanks to Jane for so much love and for punching me in the kidneys when I get lazy, my family for teaching me to read and light fires, my friends for walking with me in madness and beauty, and Contemporary Press, for publishing this story.

The Price of a Bullet by Chance Clark

To Mom and Dad for their stellar support over the years; my wife for saying yes that day on the beach; Alex for all that wicked gravy filling his cranium; my daughter, Aspyn, for keeping me so childish; and, of course, the crew at Contemporary Press for injecting lurid-ness back into pulp. I thank you all with a drooling grin.

CONTENTS

Balls

BY TONY O'NEILL

"You *seriously* expect me to let you stick that filthy thing in me?"

That was what started the whole thing. Sarah was Joe's girl-friend, and she was staying with him at the Motel 6 in East Hollywood. When the writing was going well, when he could sell pieces, when the checks were coming in, he lived there. When the writing was going badly, when there was nothing but rejection letters and unreturned phone calls, he lived in his battered eggshell-blue Volvo station wagon. He was out of the motel in two days unless he could finish his article on Rob Thomas's new album. His first attempt at evaluating the ex-Matchbox 20 front man's solo effort was flatly rejected with the note, "You cannot call Rob Thomas either a child molester or a shit-eating scumbag. Please revise." It was disgusting, hack-writing work, and it made his blood boil to even do it, but without it, Joe would starve. He carted around several full-length autobiographical books in his suitcase that mainstream publishing houses wouldn't even piss on. He thought that they were easily as good as Hemingway when he could still cut the shit, but Joe couldn't seem to get them past the nose-picking intern vetting the scripts at the first level of any serious publishing house.

All he wanted was a goddamn lay, but Sarah looked at him standing before the bed waving his erect prick at her like some kind of vague threat and balked.

"When was the last time you showered?" she asked, her eyes slitting.

"Aw Jesus, Sarah, come on! Let's do it, baby!"

"And those toenails! Jesus, you look like a homeless person, Joe. You smell like one, too. Would it really be so much effort to get a haircut, shave, maybe wash yourself, and cut those fucking *talons* before you try and lay me? Huh?"

"Christ, Sarah!" He spun around dramatically, clicking the TV off. "You gotta stop watching those *Queer Eye* fruits! All that TV's making you soft in the head. I'm a man's man, baby. That's what you like about me. You don't want me coming at you smelling like a chick—all soft and smooth."

"*Oh*," she sneered, "the *man's man*! Listen Joe ... if you were such a man, you wouldn't be having to move back into your fuckin' car next week. You'd be making the big bucks, baby! If you wanna get laid, *man's man*, you'd better *find* a man willing to let you screw him, 'cause you ain't putting that filthy, useless thing inside of me!"

It was always something with women. Sarah had been around for a few months, an Alvarado Street lush he had seen at the bar a few times. When they had started talking, she pulled out some pictures of her dopey looking kids and cursed out "that faggot ex-husband" of hers who had custody of them. But after a few more whiskey sours, she had loosened up, and they have been living together on and off ever since. Women were like drugs. When you have them around, you spend all of your time wishing they weren't there. But when they ain't around, you spend all of your time wanting them. Joe couldn't win—he half-heartedly wished he *was* a fag sometimes, so at least he wouldn't have to endure the arguments spawned from men and women's basic psychological incompatibilities. But Joe was no more a fag than he was a success. Once again, he cursed the God that had created him in such a careless fashion.

He left to get a drink. It was easier to stay away from the dealers on Alvarado as time went on. Still, he always absently fantasized about scoring some dope. It had been a couple of years since he cleaned up the last time, and this was a record. He boozed more than ever, but he was in better health and more productive than in the old days. And it was nice having a prick that worked, at least most of the time.

Leaving the liquor store with a half-pint of cheap, bottom shelf whiskey and a six-pack of Natural Light, he was accosted by a hooker he hadn't seen around the neighborhood before. She seemed to make a beeline for him, as if she had been waiting for him and him only.

"Hey," she said. "Lookin' for a party?"

She was young, Latino, pretty. He figured she was either using crack or heroin—it was a rare girl on this strip that wasn't working to feed a monkey of some description—but Joe felt that she hadn't been strung out for long. There was still something *alive* about the girl's eyes. Her hair was cut short and her eyes were dark and wide. There was something insolent about her face, and Joe liked that. Still ... Joe raised his palms. "Sorry ..."

"Wha'?" she grinned. "You homo?" Then she stepped back so he could get a better look at her body in the early evening light. She looked at him with steely determination.

"Unfortunately, no," he said, sticking the brown paper bag under his arm and reaching his other hand towards her. "Let's go. I'm right up here."

Sarah was still inside the room. He could hear the TV blaring through the door of number 63. The girl, who told Joe her name was Maria, stood mutely as he fumbled for the keys. He opened the door and marched in with the booze and the prostitute.

"Honey," he announced, "I'm home."

Sarah was still lounging on the bed. She looked up from her copy of the *LA Weekly* and asked, "And just who the fuck is this?"

"This is Maria," Joe said flatly. "I'm gonna give her money to have sex with me. Do you mind splitting for an hour or so?"

In ten minutes, Sarah had collected most of her things, cursing Joe and Maria violently as she did so. Maria sat on the bed, watching her with a bored expression. At first, Joe tried to help Sarah pack, but she looked at him and actually growled like a tiger about to spring into action when he picked up her makeup case, so now he just loitered, watching the clock on the local news channel.

"Sorry about this," he said to Maria.

"Is okay. You my last today. No rush."

When she was done, Sarah stood and looked Joe in the eye.

"*Motherfucker*," she hissed. "You better watch your back, cocksucker. You're gonna pay this little spic whore to fuck you? What about all the times I put out for you, huh? Where's my goddamned pay? Where's my pay for listening to your shit and smelling your goddamned stink and looking at your useless, dopey face? Huh?"

Joe gave her a can of Natural Light and said, "There you go."

***

Sex with Maria was easy in the way that sex with any whore is. He could tell her exactly what to do and not worry about her saying, "no." He could comment on her round ass without worrying about her suddenly freaking out about her ass being too big. Everything was reduced to a neat, clean, financial transaction. Nobody said "no" unless the money ran out. When they were done, Maria poured some whiskey and they drank in silence. Joe drained his glass and looked at her.

"I guess you gotta split, huh?" he said, slipping the bills towards her.

"Mnnnnnmmm mnm mmnmnmn mnmnmmm." The girl replied.

"*What*?" asked Joe, but his voice seemed to reverberate from a thousand miles away, coming to him in waves. Maria was looking at him with a detached, curious expression on her face. Immediately, Joe realized that he had been drugged by this prostitute when she poured the drinks, obviously for the purpose of robbing him. His last thought before everything went grey was, *Aw Jesus, not again.*

***

Sunlight streamed in through the open window. Joe's head felt like a shrapnel bomb had just erupted inside of it, spraying his brain and the inside of his skull with burning hot pieces of twisted metal. He had been out for quite a while, and the first thing he noticed was that he was almost naked. The second thing was a dull ache in his groin. And the third and most worrying thing was the blood which had seeped through his white boxer shorts and all over the bed he was passed out on. He staggered to the bathroom, and under the blinking fluorescent light, gingerly unpeeled his underwear from his body.

"Aw fuck, no," he half sobbed.

Where his balls used to be, there was an ugly, red wound, sewn up and sealed with metal surgical staples. What was left of his genitals looked bizarre and obscenely out of shape. His prick was swollen to twice its regular size from the trauma of the surgery. Joe had been butchered by the whore, or by her accomplices. He steadied himself by the sink as a shooting pain erupted from the place where his balls used to hang. He wadded wet toilet paper around the wound and staggered to get dressed.

In Duane Reed, he bought bandages and antibacterial rubs. He looked under the Pain section, but found nothing stronger than ibuprofen. The old white pharmacist informed him that if he wanted anything stronger than Tylenol, he would need an RX from a doctor.

"I don't have health insurance, and I'm in quite a lot of pain," Joe said through gritted teeth.

"Well, I'd advise getting some health insurance, then. Good day."

Instead, Joe walked an extra block and scored a bag of heroin and a rig. The dealers welcomed his return with a malevolent indifference. It was as if he'd never been away. In the room, he fixed a small amount of the heroin and felt better immediately. The pain was still there, but it was manageable. The process of cooking and shooting the drugs felt awkward and alien after so much time away. As soon as he withdrew the needle, though, he knew the next time would be a breeze. *Thank God for heroin*, Joe thought absently, the only pain control available to those of us without jobs.

He considered walking to the emergency room, but realized that his finances would not allow such a visit. He was unable to collect Medicaid, as he was technically self-employed. Joe just went through life hoping that he would never need medical assistance.

Once the pain was under control, he was able to think straight. He would have to find that whore and get his balls back. Maybe if the mutilating bitch had at least kept them on ice, they could reattach them.

Sitting in the dingy motel room with the curtains drawn, nodding on his first hit of smack in two years, waiting for the sun to set and the prostitutes to appear like roaches, Joe half-heartedly attempted to finish his freelance piece on the album. The words came, ponderous and slow, but reliable. Steady. Almost without any thought on Joe's part, the review appeared on the outsized, outdated, black and white laptop's screen. Going against his usual instincts, Joe gave the piece a thorough spell check. The words onscreen inspired nothing in him except a mild curiosity. The half-hearted praise for this banal album seemed almost channeled from some outside source. He logged on to his email account and sent the piece, thirty minutes to deadline.

A hammering at the door stirred him sometime later.

"Hey, fuck face!" screamed Sarah, slurring and drunk in the hallway. "You got any whores in there?"

"It's open."

She toppled into the room clutching a bottle of cheap fortified wine on rickety, plastic high heels.

"You've got a lot of nerve, fucko," she sneered upon seeing Joe. "A lot of fucking nerve. Who d'you think you are? Jude-fucking-Law or something? You really think you're someone special, huh?"

"No," Joe heard himself reply with genuine humility in his voice. That threw Sarah off her stride a little.

"Well ... that's right, asshole," she spluttered. "You're no one. NO ONE. A lazy, drunken, filthy NO ONE!"

"You're absolutely right, Sarah," the voice said again with what sounded like a strangulated sob at the end.

"Thinking you're the big lover man, bringing back some herpes-ridden crack whore! You're a useless, unfeeling prick!" she spat, though with a little less venom now.

"I know. I don't know what to say to you, Sarah. I'm an asshole and I'm sorry."

Sarah stopped and looked Joe up and down quizzically.

"Well ... I have a date ... but ... maybe later ..." She stopped on her way out. "I don't know what's different about you, Joe ... but I *like* it. You know where to find me."

And then she was gone.

Fortifying himself with another shot of heroin, Joe wandered Alvarado Street like a shell-shocked veteran, looking for the whore who had removed his balls. She was nowhere to be seen. None of Joe's old dealers recognized the description of the girl.

"Why you want this beetch?" enquired Paco, mouth full of wraps of cocaine on Bonnie Brae.

"She has some things that belong to me," Joe replied before dejectedly returning to his room.

That evening, an email from the editor at the music paper awaited him. They loved the piece. Payment would be dispatched immediately. If he could keep up this kind of concise, skillful writing, there were plenty more jobs for the taking. Would he be interested in writing a piece on the latest, hot New Country artist Dwain McCreedy? Not for the first time, Joe considered the possibility that the whole world apart from him was insane, before accepting the money gratefully. Someone rapped on the door frantically. Joe pulled it open.

"Sarah," he said as she walked in.

"Don't say a word, Joe. Don't say a word."

She was drunk and trying to be sexy and dramatic. This usually irritated the hell out of him. She acted like some dreadful actress in a daytime soap opera when she got like this. Except tonight it didn't bother Joe so much. He watched her with a passive interest. She raised a finger to her drunken, smeared lips.

"*Sit down.*"

He sat on the edge of the bed and started tugging at his trousers. Suddenly remembering his balls, he tried to fight her off.

"Jesus, Sarah! Let go, goddamnit!"

But she was drunk and determined, and Joe was no match for her. With a tug, down came the trousers, and then the shorts. No one spoke for a long time.

"*Jesus*, Joe!" Sarah gasped eventually. "Where are your balls?"

Joe looked dejected and shrugged his shoulders.

"Gone. Disappeared into the night. I don't think they're coming back."

They both considered this for a while.

"Does he still work?" asked Sarah, pointing to his inert prick.

"I think so."

"Hmm."

Sarah started working his soft dick with her mouth, and lo and behold, it started to get hard. The pain from the scar was less now. Joe drifted into a dreamlike state watching Sarah suck on his cock. She stopped and looked up at him with a smile.

"Let's not fight anymore," she said. "I love you, baby ..."

"I love you too, Sarah," Joe heard himself reply from far away.

***

It was summer, and life was good. Joe had an agent now. Her name was Jennifer, and she spoke with an affected accent and laughed like a chipmunk and had her WASP-y features accented with expensive plastic surgery. Now that things were going well, Joe lived at the Château Marmont. Sarah was long gone, and Joe now lived with a Tai Chi instructor named Lilly. He finally destroyed the old manuscripts he had been carrying around in the suitcase. He didn't miss them once the ashes blew away into the perfect California dusk. He had given up both alcohol and drugs and required no pain control now that the wound had healed up entirely. It was as if his balls had never been there. He looked out over his balcony as he talked to Jennifer on the cordless.

"Good news, Joe," she told him. "Doubleday agreed to upping the advance. We have a deal."

"That's wonderful, Jennifer. Thank you for calling."

"That's no problem, Joe. You just keep doing what you're doing."

"The new book will be ready before deadline."

"Is it as great as the others?"

"Well ..." Joe replied dreamily, "I can't answer, really. I guess so. It's the kind of thing that people like to read I guess. I mean it isn't going to set the world on fire but ... it's exactly like the others I suppose."

"*Wonderful*!"

Joe hung up and returned his gaze to the perfect, unchanging, baby-blue sky. Outside, cars honked and people screamed at each other in the street, driven insane by the heat and tarmac and the noise of humanity. In the pool, a young woman dived in and sailed under the water like a vast, shimmering undersea creature. Joe smiled in an odd way content for the first time in his life. He flicked on the TV.

Bundy Is a God

BY JON MCCARRON

It's widely accepted that serial killers are cunning individuals with movie star looks who secrete charismatic pheromones from highly specialized glands reserved strictly for the truly psychopathic. Once set on their unholy quests to spill innocent blood they can only be stopped by the lone work of a dogged detective with substance abuse issues—preferably in the Third Act, replete with sardonic rejoinders, as the two engage in their cat-and-mouse endgame.

This, of course, is utter horseshit.

In reality, serial killers are sad individuals with dissociative disorders, which render them incapable of forming normal human relationships, which then only serve to further reinforce the causal disorder's manifestations. Usually, the subject has experienced one or more traumatic events in the formative years of life, the most common type being sexual molestation. The molestation can then lead to questions of sexual identity, which, again, exacerbate feelings of alienation. In short, these poor souls are fucked. Literally.

However, none of this applies to Lewis Newburg. He's not an

unhappy man. And while he doesn't generally like people, he rarely thinks of them as moving flesh bags. At least, he doesn't when he takes his meds. As to molestation, there was none in his history to speak of, unless, of course, you count the occasions when he was forced to suck off his stepfather. Which he doesn't. If that was molestation, Lewis reasons, he would have negative feelings about the experiences. Not that he had enjoyed burying his nose in his mother's husband's pubic hair and receiving the coppery taste in his mouth at the end, whereupon he'd be shoved away in disgust. As he's fond of telling the men who strike up conversations at the bars he frequents: "I ain't queer." Why couldn't these fags understand he was just there because the drinks were cheap? Besides, he rarely achieves orgasm when he has sex with men, so how could he possibly be a homosexual?

No, becoming a serial killer was strictly a career move. Serial killers enjoy national attention. Newspapers speculate as to the murderer's identity. Radio talk show hosts blather endlessly about the gory minutiae and take the ninth caller for tickets to Ozzfest. As his mother's husband had told him once as he wiped semen from Lewis's cheek: "There's no such thing as bad attention." In the beating that followed, Lewis found comfort in these words and coddled the warm numbness growing inside him. Worst case scenario? A serial killer gets caught and the public finally puts a face to the body of work. From there the possibilities are endless. Interviews. Book deals. Throngs of women who write daily, cry for clemency, and propose marriage.

Most of these women are fat.

Moped jokes aside, Lewis figured he could steel himself to fuck a fat woman. That Lewis himself is fat strikes no chord of hypocrisy within him. He is, after all, the sole perfect expression of the universe.

The key to this fame is of course being caught. Everyone knows who Ted Bundy was, but ask about the Zodiac Killer and you'll get a blank look. Even those familiar with his crimes still can only postulate as to his true identity decades later. He's either dead or locked up on an unrelated offense.

Lewis has done his research, studying the Zodiac's work and much-ballyhooed arcane cryptograms. In the end, he discarded it all. The man was either crazy or unwilling to be apprehended, which to Lewis is the real lunacy. What good is a serial killer whose name is never known? Bundy's eloquence and All-American looks, coupled with his rapes, made him (for lack of a better term) sexy to the media and the American public. Beyond that, Bundy had been brought down by good old-fashioned police work. Berkowitz was caught because of parking tickets. A common scofflaw. John Wayne Gacy was arrested after investigators noticed a strange odor emanating from his house. The source was eventually revealed to be the decomposing nude bodies of twenty-nine young men and boys. Distasteful. One shouldn't shit where one eats. Besides, full Christian names are for assassins.

As such, it's clear that being caught isn't enough. One must be caught in a palatable manner with the requisite trial publicity. In this respect, you had to hand it to Bundy. Even the presiding judge offered that he would have been honored to have seen him at work—in a legal capacity, mind you. Unofficial reports indicate that Bundy died sporting an erection. An uncredited source on the body reclamation team is said to have remarked, "He done rode all them bitches, but even Ol' Sparky couldn't tax that hard-on." Again, this is all unsubstantiated and not recorded in the attending physician's notes, but Lewis still thinks about it occasionally while masturbating, wishing it true.

In the end, Bundy wasn't perfect. He'd been caught, but not

because he'd wanted to be. That was his one failing. Lewis knows in his heart that he can do better.

These are Lewis's most private thoughts and dreams, and I alone am privy to them. As sad as his tale is, there are times I pity myself even more for one reason—he's my Thursday two o'clock.

Lord, give me strength.

***

As if his plight wasn't pathetic enough, the poor bastard has failings of his own that surpass all that we've covered so far. This man, this engine of quiet rage and indifference to the suffering of others, is totally and completely incapable of harming a soul.

You see, he can't stand confrontation.

As a highly ritualized sociopath, Lewis has bought into the Hollywood stereotype of papier-mâché victims who fold at an attacker's first blow or expire upon receiving a single stab wound. For years, he enjoyed endless thrillers in which the villains harvested their prey with a cold demeanor as easily as you or I might mop a floor. However, he is frustrated by the recent trend in slasher movies of featuring less-than-helpless victims—Lewis's most vexing examples being the *Scream* trilogy—who pummel their attacker and occasionally escape danger. He brought this up in one of our sessions.

"So I was watching a movie the other night. *Scream*. You ever see it?"

I allowed that I had indeed seen it. I have a bit of a thing for Rose McGowan. As this was immaterial, I omitted this fact, but I mention it here because she really is easy on the eyes.

"It was okay at first. The opening was great. The way that blonde bitch died choking on her own blood, strung up in a tree with her intestines spilling out. Good stuff. But then it started to bother me. The thing was ... why didn't the rest of those bitches die, too? I mean, the Scream guy kept coming at them, but they kept on punching and kicking him. They could have hurt him."

"It's just a movie, Lewis," I told him.

"Yeah, but it wasn't even believable."

I let this comment pass. If I took the time to point out every single disconnect Lewis had, we'd never get anywhere. Pick your battles, a colleague once told me. I didn't even have to watch *Dr. Phil* to learn that shit.

When it became apparent I wasn't going to remark, Lewis continued.

"The Scream guy should have been able to kill them easier than that. I bet that really pissed him off. The way they fought back."

"It's part of our human nature, Lewis. People fight to stay alive. Wouldn't you?" It was out before I could stop myself.

"Well, yeah," he replied in his usual are-you-stupid tone. "But then, I'm not a bag of flesh."

I made a note to up his Seroquel.

In a follow-up session we explored the idea of confrontation and the failure of reality to live up to ideation. Two days previous, Lewis had been in a grocery store. After the clerk rang up his box of bandages and razors, he gave Lewis the total. While digging in his pocket for change, Lewis noticed his shoe was untied. Again, being a slave to ritual, Lewis dropped the contents of his pocket on the counter and bent to tie his laces. When he stood back up, the cashier had placed the money in the register and stated that Lewis was fifty-three cents short. This stopped Lewis in his tracks. He told the clerk he'd already given him all the money required for the purchase. The clerk sighed (this irked Lewis to no end) and informed him that the line was long, and if he didn't have the fifty-three cents, he'd have to place the items back on their shelves.

Individuals who thrive on ritual can get easily thrown by obstacles. The ensuing reaction can vary in severity from mild disorientation to extreme agitation. Lewis's reaction was somewhere in the neighborhood of telling Ann Coulter that abortions tickle.

"That little cocksucker. I was so mad! I gave him all the money I had on me and he fucking LIED to my FACE!"

"How did that make you feel?" I asked. Yes, sometimes therapist's questions really are this banal. You learn to deal with it.

"I wanted to cut his face off with a grapefruit spoon. I wanted to gut him in front of the whole fucking store and dance in his blood as it sprayed all over me."

"Why? What end would you hope to achieve by doing this?"

"Well. Maybe then he'd take me seriously next time."

I made a note to up *my* Seroquel.

"Alright, Lewis. If you felt this way, why didn't you do it?"

At this point, a therapist would hope for a breakthrough like, "It would be wrong," or, "I would have gone to jail."

Lewis meekly replied, "Because he was looking at me. In the eyes. And I just knew he'd seen that *Scream* movie. And *he* knew he didn't have to die just because I wanted it."

Alert the press! A horror movie prevented a homicide!

In subsequent sessions this theme was played and replayed— the incident with his neighbor's loud rap music; the woman who stole the cab he had flagged down, and so on and so on. Every time he reached down inside himself to unchain The Beast, it scurried away at the first sign of conflict. His reconciliations of these events versus their outcomes were as convoluted as they were imaginative.

"If I'd pushed her under the bus they'd've done a news story on me. Being famous, I could hardly sneak up on someone and kill them. They'd be like, "Hey! You're the guy from the news!" and then buy me a drink or something."

"If I'd tied razor-wire around his neck like I wanted to, I'd have been late to the theater and traffic is a bitch after five and you *know* I like the previews."

I nodded. I like the previews too.

Moreover, Lewis is deathly afraid of blood. Most of the time he sports a ragged beard. He nicked himself shaving once and ended up calling 9-1-1. The EMTs had to immobilize him in three-point restraints because he was so hysterical. After he stopped struggling, he tearfully begged the EMTs not to cut off his penis. He was *that* out of it from seeing the sight of his own blood.

I can't make this stuff up.

His final obstacle in the ultimate goal of becoming a world-renowned boogeyman was his inability to make a decision.

"I just can't decide. I mean every killer has an M.O. *Modus Operandi*. Do you know what that means?"

I assured Lewis that while my Latin was rusty, I have been on a sales conference or two in my time.

"Choosing an M.O. is hard. It has to say who I am. What am I about? What's my message to my fans?"

That you're a fucking moron, I thought.

"I don't know. What was Bundy's message; I'm horny?" I asked, smiling.

That got Lewis going.

"Don't talk about Bundy that way. He was a genius. We still haven't figured his message out. But when we do, it'll change the world."

"We?" I asked.

"His children. The disciples of dispatch. We aren't organized or anything. I'm not crazy, so stop looking at me that way. I'm just saying. There's plenty of people who dug him. That's all I'm saying."

I nodded sagely and jotted down a note to myself that Disciples of Dispatch is a good band name. Hey, you have to look busy or people start feeling ripped-off.

"But if you're the sole manifestation of the universe, why would you count yourself among their numbers?"

Lewis thought about this a moment and said one of the sanest things I had heard him utter to date.

"Shut up."

After getting him back on track, he confided that he'd had no small difficulty in ascertaining the M.O. for his work.

"At first I thought about being the Fibonacci Killer. You know, base the dates of my kills on the Fibonacci sequence. My first kill on January 1, my second on February 1, my third on March 2, my fourth on April 3, my fifth on May 5 ... just like the number progression: 1, 1, 2, 3, 5 ... but then I realized that the pattern would only last eight iterations."

Familiar with the numerical progression, which consists of adding the current number to the previous number to arrive at a subsequent number for further addition, I saw the problem. The eighth and final murder would leave him at August 21, since there's no September 34. Keeping in mind that Lewis needs structure and ritual, it's easy to see how this could be off-putting. He wouldn't even be able to complete a year's cycle. And beyond that, it was needlessly complex. Most of the public wouldn't even know who the hell Fibonacci was, let alone know anything about his work with predictable patterning in nature. Besides, it smacked of *The Da Vinci Code*, and who the fuck wants to be associated with that except Tom Hanks, who hasn't been entertaining since *"Bosom Buddies"?* Moreover, this all missed the bigger issue at hand: how did this idiot learn the word "iteration?"

Lewis's next idea was to work only with prime numbers. One murder per month, committed on the next occurring date which is a prime number.

"It's perfect!" Lewis was near tears. "I know it's a sign now! This is gonna be my talking dog! There's twelve primes between one and thirty-one and there's twelve months in a year! I can't wait!"

He actually cheered up for a few sessions. He'd finally worked this bitch of a kernel out from his gumline and wanted everyone to know about it. And like I said, it lasted a few memorable weeks.

Then someone went and pissed all over his parade.

I knew it was a bad day when Lewis showed up wearing his Morrissey t-shirt. He only wears that shirt when it's a blue Monday (or Thursday for that matter).

"My life is over," he moaned. "It has no meaning and I might as well die."

I remained silent, not sure if he was actually beginning a conversation or quoting some Morrissey ditty. I'm admittedly ignorant of the man's music, preferring, say, good music. Like Grand Funk.

"The prime numbers aren't going to work out after all."

"What do you mean?" I asked, genuinely puzzled.

He couldn't even look at me.

"There are thirteen primes between one and thirty-one. I forgot to count two. It's the only even prime there is. I FUCKING FORGOT THE NUMBER TWO!" he screamed. "Now there's no pattern once again and I'm back to square one!"

If it had been anyone else I might have been concerned for my personal safety.

"I'm sorry this has upset you, Lewis. I can see how much you wanted this to work out."

"But this was supposed to be my talking dog!"

"If it's any consolation, Lewis, Berkowitz didn't really hear his dog telling him to do things. Most people don't know this, but after Agent John Douglas harangued Berkowitz about the ludicrous nature of his dog alibi, the mighty Son of Sam gave it up and admitted the whole thing was bullshit."

Lewis took this in. Finally, he shook his head and said, "You're just trying to make me feel better."

"Yes, I am trying to make you feel better. But it's still true. Douglas ended up being the father of the profiling movement. You can Google it."

After a few beats Lewis looked up at me and smiled slightly.

"Thanks," he said.

That night I left my office feeling like I'd actually accomplished something for once.

Three hours later, Lewis attempted suicide.

A week after being released from County, we met again in my office. He'd wanted to meet sooner but, again, he was my Thursday two o'clock. Offering him another slot was simply not an option.

"So. Lewis. I'm told you informed the admitting nurse that you've been off your meds for some time. I thought we'd talked about this."

"*You* talked about it. I told you it makes me feel like I'm wrapped in plastic."

His voice was still the tiniest bit weak. Nooses do that.

"You have no idea what it's like not being able to think straight, having all these thoughts just interrupting and second-guessing!" He winced slightly as his pitch rose.

These "thoughts" are what normal people call a conscience. Super Ego. Morals. Pick your terminology; it's the same song.

I sighed.

"The reason I agreed to see you today, Lewis, is that I'm afraid we've reached an impasse. We've learned all we can from each other, which, I'm sad to say, hasn't been substantial enough to continue justifying the pressure it's placed on either of us. I've spent the last week trying to see another way through this, but I can't."

Lewis snapped his attention back to me.

"You're dumping me?" He was incredulous. "You're supposed to help me!" Wince.

"I've tried, Lewis. However, in the end I don't think I was ready for someone with, well, a case history like yours. I'm referring you to a friend of mine. She's an excellent therapist who is much more well-trained in dealing with ..."

"Psychos, right?"

"You're not psychotic, Lewis. You're probably sociopathic. Further probing might even indicate that you have some high-functioning form of Asperger's syndrome. All I know is that I can't be there for that diagnosis. You've placed an enormous strain on our relationship. Therapy is more intensive than a career and more intimate than friendship. You have to trust me to be there when you need me. And I have to trust that you trust me to be there. You left this office two weeks ago with me thinking I'd made some headway. Do you have any idea how I felt when I found out that you'd tried to kill yourself? It was a violation. And it was unacceptable. I simply can't work in an atmosphere like this anymore. Dr. Redding is better-equipped than I am to help you through all this."

The next twenty minutes were a combination of Lewis screaming at me, me screaming at Lewis, and Lewis screaming at no one in particular. In one of his lulls, catching his breath and clutching at his raw throat, I glanced at my watch.

Shit! I had less than half an hour to get across town. It was my day to pick Meghan up from school and I couldn't be a single minute late. Cheerleading had been cancelled tonight, and if I didn't show, she'd have to walk home.

"I'm sorry, Lewis, but we're done here. I have a previous engagement."

"Oh! So you have time for some other crazy but not me, who desperately needs your help!"

I couldn't win.

"I won't be charging you for this visit, Lewis. See Lisa on your way out. She'll set you up with Dr. Redding's schedule, and I may even check in on your progress. From a distance. Either way, I'm afraid it's time to leave. Our time is up."

Lewis jumped up and kicked his chair over. He stormed out of my office and past my secretary, kicking out part of the glass-paneled door on his way to the street.

I stood for a moment, stunned.

I'd provoked a reaction.

I'd actually goaded him into reacting. Violently.

His fear of confrontation seemed to be weakening. For a moment I was surprised. And elated. Only later would I consider if this had been a good thing. But that was later.

I rushed past Lisa, yelling back for her to call the super and have the door fixed as soon as possible. Moments later, I peeled into the parking lot of St. Charles Primary.

With seconds to spare, I saw Meghan come running out of the front doors. I smiled with no small pride at her innocence. So happy. So untouched.

She'd never know the nightmares I dealt with on a daily basis. The horrors I calmly labeled from the safety of a DSM. I wanted to protect her as long as I could. But that's the thing about kids. They grow up. They eventually tear the gauze from their eyes and see the world as we grownups have made it.

I'm sorry, baby.

She saw my van and brightened, pumping her tiny legs as fast as she could.

"UNCLE DAN!" she screamed.

I reached across the console and opened the passenger door for her. She jumped in and yanked it shut as we pulled away, a thousand soccer moms queuing behind me.

"How was school today, Meghan?"

"It was okay. Andy Jeffries brought a snake to class."

I made a face. "Gross."

"No! It was cool! I like snakes now. But then it pooped." She mimicked my expression.

"What else happened today?" I flicked on my left blinker. The expressway was supposed to be a mess for the next three weeks.

"Um ... nothing. But yesterday Carrie and Jesse said they're having a double slumber party for their birthdays next month."

"And you were invited?"

"No. I don't like them. They're stuck-up. But mom said she'd see that I could go. I don't really care."

"Well, I don't think you should go if you don't really want to. Never make a priority of someone to whom you yourself aren't a priority."

"What's that mean?"

"It means nuts to them broads," I winked.

"You talk funny, Uncle Dan," Meghan giggled.

"That I do."

I switched my blinker on again and hung a right at Lapeer.

Meghan turned back to the road.

"Are we going to the movies again? You missed my road, DanMan."

DanMan. That always made me smile.

"I'm afraid not, precious. I spoke to your dad again today."

Meghan was all ears.

"Daddeeee? What did he say, DanMan? Did he say hi and he loves me?"

"You know he did!" I smiled. "But he also told me he knows your mom isn't feeling well. He's sorry he can't be here, but he promises to come home real soon if you're good for your mom. That said, he decided that mom needs a night off. Just for herself. Do you ever feel that way? When you just want the world to leave you alone so you can just think?"

Meghan thought for a moment. Then she shook her head.

I laughed.

"Well, maybe you're a bit young to worry about that kind of stuff."

"I'm almost twelve!" she cried indignantly, mock-slapping at me.

"So you are. My mistake, my queen! Seriously, though. Your mom is kind of unfocused right now. She needs to work on herself. She needs to find a center and figure out how to talk about her problems. And if you can help with that I know she'll love you even more than she does now."

We made another left.

"Better put your seatbelt on, sweetheart. This is a safety car and we obey the rules of the road."

She nodded and clipped the metal tongue into place.

"So then, where are we going?" she finally got around to asking.

"Well ... I'm not supposed to say ..." I stalled.

"DaaaanMaaannnnn!"

I covered my ears in jest.

"Okay, okay! Well, you can't say anything. He wanted it to be a surprise. But your dad's ship is in town for just *one hour*. He talked to his captain and he okayed us coming on board. You'll even get to see where your dad works!"

Meghan was near tears as we drove down to the docks.

"Daddy," she whispered. It was all she could say.

I smiled and cut the power to the automatic locks.

I'm betting Meghan's mother will have plenty to talk about at her next session.

Happy, Happy Yumi-Chan

BY JASON WILLIAM MCNEIL

People always asked Yumiko why she was sad. "A pretty girl like you," they'd say, "should be smiling. Come on and smile for us, Yumi-chan."

First of all, who the hell gave them permission to tack the very familiar, too-affectionate "-chan" onto her name, like they were family or something, and secondly, why the hell did they care whether she flexed her facial muscles one way or the other? Sometimes she'd plaster on a big, fake grin just to shut them up. More often, though, she'd just harden her already sullen stare, her dark almond eyes staring out, half-hidden from behind straight, black bangs, and that would shut them up for a while, at least.

"Cheer up, sweetie." She heard that one a lot, too, and "It can't be as bad as all that." Just because she didn't skip around the mega-mall, chattering and giggling like some vapid *ko-gal*, adults seemed genuinely alarmed. The prospect of an unhappy Japanese schoolgirl, she thought, must threaten their carefully crafted delusions of reality.

Whatever. Truth was Yumiko didn't feel sad at all. She didn't feel depressed, despondent, or any of the other hundred or so synonyms for "having a shitty day, thank you very much." Neither did she feel happy, or anxious, or infatuated, or even peckish, or any of the other ways that people said they felt. Truth was, most of the time Yumiko Tanaka didn't feel much of anything at all.

For as many of her sixteen years as she could remember, Yumi felt disconnected from the rest of the world, or at least from the rest of the people in it. She was immune to emotional highs and lows. She carried no warm and fuzzy memories of childhood loved ones. Never nursed any girlhood crushes on J-Pop boy band singers, like all her classmates. Never giggled with delight over a pet puppy, or even laughed at one of the ridiculous TV game shows that her Nipponese countrymen seem to churn out even faster than microchips. Nothing. Nothing at all. When her mother died shortly after Yumiko's sixth birthday, the little girl didn't understand what all the boo-hooing was about. If Mommy really was in a better place, like the *Kiristan* priest said at the funeral, then what was there to be sad about? Sure, life would be different now, but that's just the way it is, so why cry? Even at six, Yumi knew she was different from other people, and had decided that most adults were probably stupid and defiantly said things they didn't believe.

For the next ten years, when her father, the "salary man," rode the weekend rails from his office in Kyoto, Yumi would dutifully meet him at the train station, ride home with him in the taxi then watch him spend his days off wallowing in loneliness and American whiskey. Every Monday morning, she would get ready for school early, then order another taxi to deliver a hung-over, bleary-eyed Mr. Tanaka to the bullet train that would take him back to Kyoto for another week of doing something she didn't care about for a company that was a subsidiary of another company whose name she could never remember. Every week, just before the yellow *takashi* pulled away, Yumiko's father would fight back tears, kiss her on the forehead, and say she looked more like her mother every day.

It all seemed pretty stupid to her; to make himself miserable weekend after weekend after weekend. When a Buddhist death cult set off a sirin gas bomb on Mr. Tanaka's Friday train home, killing him and everyone else in the business class commuter car, Yumi figured it was probably for the best. Whether her old man was finally in a better place with mother (which she doubted) or was simply cold, dead, and gone, at least his misery was over. At the very least, she wouldn't have to clean up after his weekend binges anymore, and she figured that had to be a good thing.

The only place Yumiko Tanaka came out of emotional neutral was at the Ryu-Kaze Dojo (Dragon Wind Martial Arts School). Sure, she'd tried booze and drugs, and had even gone through a phase of much illicit sex with boys and old men and even a few girls, but nothing ever made her feel really alive until she began training at the dojo. From her very first lesson, Yumi was hooked on the elegant carnage of the ancient fighting arts. First two and three times a week, then finally five and sometimes six nights in a row, Yumi would rush from school to the little tile-roofed training hall with the white, half-timbered walls and spotless, hardwood floor. There, she would trade her blue and green school uniform for a white cotton *gi* and engage in an exercise of ritualized violence.

Make no mistake; it was the violence that she craved. Sure, her teacher, Horiuchi-sensei, made much of the notion that "the martial arts are for defense only" and "we train to forge our bodies and discipline our minds" and all those fortune cookie clichés that pass for dojo wisdom, but Yumi figured that her sensei was just one more example of an adult spouting high-sounding platitudes he really didn't believe, just trying to talk himself into a truth his heart knew was false.

Yumiko knew better. She knew that the samurai arts were developed by warriors who killed and died without remorse, without hesitation, without thought. "The way of the samurai is death" said the first words of the *Hagakure*, the medieval manual of moral instruction to Japan's warrior elite, not "The way of the samurai is for defense only" or "The way of the samurai is to forge our bodies and discipline our minds." Death. Violence. Bloodshed raised to the level of fine art. Other students came to the Ryu-Kaze Dojo looking for peace, or serenity, or confidence, or any number of other bullshit philosophical goals. Yumi just liked kicking ass. Not only did she like it, she was good at it. Night after night, she showed both talent and enthusiasm for the ancient and honorable ways of dealing death.

Yumi loved everything about the ritualized combat of the dojo: the sweaty uniform, the clack of wooden weapons, the sting of a bamboo *shinai* (practice sword) when she failed to block a sparring partner's attack, the yelp and subsequent THUD as a perfectly executed *aikijujitsu* throw sent her opponent flying high then crumpling into a heap on the unforgiving floor and most of all, the satisfying crunch of a classmate's ribs on the receiving end of a stomping side kick. She wasn't sure if she felt a connection to her samurai ancestors, or felt pride in her rapid mastery of their battle-born skills, but she knew that she felt something when she punched and kicked and hacked and slashed her way through the sensei's nightly pantomime of battlefield carnage, and that was enough for Yumiko.

As she rose through the Ryu-Kaze ranks to become *uke-deshi*, or "favored student," Yumi felt more and more like the rest of her waking hours were nothing but a dull, numb blur, and the only time she sprang fully to life was on the dojo floor, moving through ancient dances of death while beating her classmates senseless.

Sensei had spoken to her several times about taking too much pleasure in aggression, but even though she did her best to hide it, the sheer glee she took from inflicting bodily harm came shining through again and again. Her thrill of victory was, with frustrating regularity, cut short by a stinging admonishment from Sensei Horiuchi. While he went on and on about "the sword that does not kill" and "seeking peace in the heart of danger," Yumi kept her eyes lowered in an expression she hoped would pass for humility. In reality, her feigned shame was a desperate effort to hide a growing contempt for her sensei's pacifist platitudes. Though she nursed a suspicion that her teacher was as naive a fool as all the others, the idea of being turned out into the street, of being denied her nightly dance with death, terrified Yumi so much that she suffered her sensei's admonishments in silence and supplication, pretending to take his pithy words to heart.

It was just such a reprimand that had kept Yumi late at the dojo after an overly enthusiastic evening of sparring nearly an hour after the last of her classmates had gone home. As she stuffed her sweaty (and now, from the incident that had so enraged the sensei, bloodstained) gi into her backpack and pulled on a painfully cute Hello Kitty t-shirt (a gift from a well-meaning but clueless auntie), Yumi heard unfamiliar voices coming from the main training hall. Curious, she peeked out from behind the sliding *shoji* screen that separated the women's changing room and saw a half-dozen men standing in a circle in the middle of the dojo floor. Although differing in the details, each wore some version of a dark, skinny-cut suit over shiny disco shirts so loud they could probably scream in four octaves. Even though the sun had long since set and, for that matter, they were all inside, each of the tough-guy fashion victims hid his eyes behind dark sunglasses. Some of them, Yumi noticed, were missing bits of fingers, while hints of inked skin peeking from behind cuff and collar promised serious tattoos beneath. "*Yakuza*," she mouthed silently. Gangsters.

In the center of this human orbit stood her sensei facing a beautiful woman, who was dressed traditionally in a fine white kimono printed with red *sakura* blossoms and wrapped with a pale pink sash. Odd clothes aside, the strangers' most noticeable accessories were the curved swords that all seven, including the pretty woman, were carrying. Incongruously, the sensei held only a *bokken*, the heavy wooden practice sword.

Holding her breath and straining to hear, Yumiko could barely make out the polite but obviously unpleasant words that passed between her teacher and the strange lady.

"You misunderstand me, venerable Sensei," said the kimono-clad woman, in a voice so low and even that she might have been discussing the falling spring blossoms. "This is not a negotiation. We are not here to collect money."

"What do you want, then?" Sensei growled through gritted teeth. Yumi could see him tightening his grip on his bokken. He was ready to fight on half a moment's notice.

"As my associates informed you before, Sensei-san, the yakuza once more have need of your skills. However, I have been told that you no longer wish to instruct the Ghost Dragons in the warrior arts. Surely," she smiled faintly and cast her eyes downward, "this rumor is false."

"As I told your predecessor a decade ago," Sensei grumbled, "I no longer teach killers. I no longer train gangsters. Let the Ghost Dragons learn killing from someone else. My sword is sheathed forever."

"Although my predecessor, as you call him, may have allowed such disloyalty from a retainer, rest assured that I will not." Though she still gazed from beneath lowered lids, the kimonoed woman's voice took on an edge that cut to the quick of Yumi's soul. "That sort of lax discipline is one reason why I am now *oyabun*—the boss of bosses—and he is resting in the trunks of four cars."

With a raise of her delicate chin, her onyx dark eyes locked with Horiuchi-sensei's. "Consider the last ten years a leave of absence that has now been rescinded. No one quits the yakuza. You are one of us for life. Like the samurai of old, the only way out is death." She stepped out of her circle of henchmen, leaving Horiuchi-sensei surrounded by sword-wielding killers.

"Please," the lady oyabun said, "reconsider."

"Go to hell."

"So be it."

Yumi's heart leapt into her throat as she heard the distinctive sound of six steel blades sliding from six wooden scabbards. Before the swords had cleared their cases, though, her sensei's bokken had sprung into a blur of destruction. One black-suited assailant fell to the ground, his sword still half-sheathed, his right ear torn and hanging free, pumping blood onto the polished wooden floor. The gangster to his left caught the second half of the sensei's first strike full in the face, and fell back cursing and spitting teeth.

Spinning around just in time to parry a sword thrust from behind, Sensei Horiuchi smacked his wooden blade hard against the would-be back-stabber's hand, breaking the coward's thumb and forcing him to drop his katana. No more gripping and holding with that hand for Number Three, at least not today

Leaping past the hoodlum with the shattered hand, he blocked and rolled away from the remaining three thugs and towards the dojo weapons rack. Yumi assumed that her teacher was looking for a better answer to four samurai swords than a blunt wooden practice stick, and expected him to snatch his five-hundred-year-old ancestral katana from its place of honor before the school's altar.

To her surprise, his leaping roll took him past the small shrine and to a brace of racked staves and pole-arms, from which he pulled a long spear that sported a nasty-looking, back-barbed hook jutting out at a right angle just below the weapon's razor-sharp steel head. Developed by a Buddhist monk with a strange passion for spear-play, the *Hozoin* spear was capable of much more in the hands of a master than the usual poke-block-stab action of more traditional spears. Yumi had seen it used in solo *kata* practice before, and even in the occasional tightly choreographed *bunkai* demonstration against another weapon, but never in combat. She knew she should be afraid for her sensei, should sneak to the phone and call the police, should do something, but the promise of more violence, ready to burst forth like a storm cloud fat with too much thunder, kept her alive. She was rapt.

As he turned to bring his spear to bear on the three pursuing Ghost Dragons, Horiuchi-sensei sent a sudden thrust flying to the face of the thug in the middle. Like an archer splitting a bull's-eyed arrow, his point shattered the black plastic and the eyeball behind it. Screaming, the middle-man dropped his sword as both hands instinctively flew to clutch at his ruined, bloody socket. A barely perceptible twitch of the spear gave the steel tip a second thrust, this time between the unfortunate gangster's ribs, ending his suffering, his life, and his short career as a Cyclops all in the space of an instant.

Sensei whipped back his spear and settled into a low defensive stance, weight on the balls of his feet, with the tip of the Hozoin spear swaying back and forth like a dancing cobra in the space between the two remaining hoods. The next move was theirs.

"Your skills are as impressive as ever, old man," the lady

oyabun called from across the room, sounding surprisingly uncon-cerned about the maiming and mortal wounds suffered by her retainers.

"Your killers are of a poorer quality than I remember," the sen-sei answered, still keeping the last two Ghost Dragons at bay with the threat of gore-covered sharpened steel swaying on the end of a two meter wooden shaft.

She smiled. "They were not trained by the great Sensei Horiuchi, as were their predecessors. Had they been, your blood would stain the floor, not theirs. It is an interesting dichotomy."

The old man snorted, "Had they stayed home tonight and left The Great Sensei Horiuchi in peace, their blood would not stain the floor, either."

"Sadly, that was not their karma," reflected the woman, almost to herself. Then, louder, she shouted, "Enough of this. Hajime, attack!"

At their mistress' command, both Ghost Dragons raised their katanas high and charged toward Horiuchi-sensei. The old man's spear thrust out again, narrowly missing Lefty's shoulder and pass-ing into the empty space between the swordsmen. For an instant, Lefty grinned wide. The old bastard had missed. But then he felt the bite of the Hozoin spear's hooked blade bite into the back of his leg.

Hooking the thug's feet from under him, Sensei's powerful arms twisted the spear's shaft and sent Lefty crashing into his right-sided compatriot. Both went down hard, smacking together like bowling pins knocked out of a seven-ten split.

Stunned, both struggled to regain their feet, only to be swept to the floor again and again by the sensei's back-hooked Buddhist spear. Pacifists or not, Yumi thought, those monks knew what they were doing when it came to tricking out pole-arms. After their third crash to the dojo floor, Lefty stood up alone. Looking down, he saw that Righty had fallen on his katana and was too busy coughing up whatever blood wasn't draining onto the hardwood to attempt another assault on the sensei. Where there had been six, Lefty now stood alone against the Master. Honor demanded victory, or death. Maybe both.

Yumi saw a strange look of resolve set into the lone Ghost Dragon's face. Letting loose an ear-splitting "Banzai," Lefty raised his sword high and leapt straight onto the old man's spear. Stunned, Yumi watched the spear tip disappear into the gangster's blood-splattered orange and blue paisley shirt and explode from the back of his black jacket. Hanging impaled on the Hozoin shaft, Lefty's sword arm slashed down in his last act on Earth, slicing deep into the sensei's right arm. Only a desperate, reflexive twist of Horiuchi-sensei's torso prevented the kamikaze katana cut from taking his arm off below the shoulder. As it was, the blade bit deep, spraying blood in a wide arc and leaving the limb all but useless. Both the spear and Lefty's corpse dropped to the floor.

From her hiding place, Yumi saw her sensei, gasping, sweating and bleeding, moving backwards to the weapons rack, taking a single, three-pronged metal *sai* from the wall with his uninjured hand. *A good choice*, Yumi thought. The sai was an Okinawan tool, used by farmers and fishermen to catch and break the swords of their samurai overlords.

Sensei took a defensive stance in the center of the dojo and gestured for the elegantly dressed lady crime boss to come to him. She obliged.

Seemingly oblivious to the carnage around her, or to the bloody defeat of a half-dozen of her retainers, the kimonoed woman moved with all the grace and delicacy of a Noh theatre performer. Her long white sleeves flowed in perfect counterpoint to the drawing of her sword. As the deadly katana slid free from its sheath, her silk robes rustled like fresh sheets on the line in a gentle spring breeze.

Yumi thought that she had never seen anything more beautiful.

The faintest of smiles played across the oyabun's rose-petal lips. "A samurai should not fight a death duel using a farmer's weapon, Horiuchi-san. You should meet your fate with your father's sword in hand."

Sensei's stance did not waver. "While you may dress up and play at being samurai, Miyagi Midori, you are nothing but yakuza scum. You are not worthy to face my family's blade."

Midori's smile withered, collapsing into a mask of murderous hatred. Knuckles whitening around her katana's braided handle, the lady oyabun's stance shifted into a coiled posture of attack. Either she or the sensei would not outlive the next minute.

"Besides," Sensei continued, as the two combatants slowly circled one another, each searching for a single moment of weakness in which to end the other's life, "as I have already explained, my sword is sheathed forever and ..."

Sensei's vow was left unfinished, cut short by the foot of sharpened, five-hundred-year-old *Muramasa* steel that burst from the center of his chest. Looking down in confusion, he dropped the sai and struggled to turn. Before his eyes clouded over in death and he went on to a better place (probably not) or just went cold and dead (obviously), the great Horiuchi-sensei's last sight on Earth was that of Yumiko Tanaka, his star pupil, staring down at him with blood-covered hands and, behind her, the empty sword stand on the dojo altar.

Funny, he thought. It was the first time he'd seen Yumi-chan smile.

Stepping over her sensei's already cooling corpse, Yumiko

tugged the ancestral sword free from his back and wiped it clean on the old man's sleeve. Picking her way between the bodies of the fallen yakuza, she crossed the ruined wooden floor to the waiting vision in white. Bare-kneed in her school skirt, Yumiko knelt in a pool of blood at Midori's feet and offered up her teacher's katana to the most beautiful killer she had ever seen.

"My lady," said Yumi, holding up the sword with both hands while bowing her head low.

Her silk robes now speckled with both cherry blossoms and gore, the oyabun took the sword of her vanquished enemy, bade the girl to rise and, without another word, the two women left the Ryu-Kaze Dojo, leaving delicate, bloody footprints behind them.

First Draft

BY CRAIG MCDONALD

The whore is dead, no question about that.

"Writing these mysteries you do, Héctor," the fat Mexican madam says, fanning herself, "you see now why I sent for you, yes?"

Héctor Lassiter squats down next to the murdered prostitute, hams on heels and head to the side, examining her body. The girl's own head is nearly twisted off. She's sprawled on her belly ... a rare enough position for a woman in her line of work, and rarer still for one with such a massive rack. Spread-eagle on her belly as she is, he shouldn't be able to see luckless Marita's lolling tongue and bulging eyes—their blood vessels all ruptured. But now the dead girl's head is turned 180-degrees, like she's checking out her own bare ass and not appreciating the view.

Poor, sweet Marita. Héctor had her a few times. She was one of the rare ones who loved her work. Even now, he can vividly conjure up what it felt like to be inside her. He's written about what *that* was like at least twice. He liked her fine.

As he always does under pressure, Héctor steps outside himself to see how he's handling it, seeking out what's sticking in his mind for later description, grasping for that single telling detail that lends an undeniable sense of truth that sells it to the reader.

Clutched in the dead girl's hand is her locket, torn from her own ruined neck. Héctor coaxes the locket and broken chain from her hand and opens it to reveal a picture of an older woman, one who resembles the dead whore around the mouth and eyes. Hopeless and facing death, Héctor figures Marita reached out for her mama, like a doomed little girl reaching for her mother's protective hand.

Héctor rises—wincing as his knees crack—and fishes his pocket for his Zippo and Pall Malls. He always plots best when smoking or behind the wheel of his Chevrolet. Héctor slits the virgin pack with a yellowed thumbnail and shakes one loose. Firing it up, he turns to Madam Ruiz. He blows smoke and asks, "Where's the boy?"

"In another room," the old, big boss whore says, curling her hairy lip. It's been twelve hours since Héctor last shaved and the shadow on Luisa Ruiz's upper lip already shames his own. "He's passed out, stinking drunk," she says.

Héctor nods. "The boy talk much after ...?" Héctor gestures at Marita's body with his cigarette.

"No, Héctor. We found her like this when the boy went twenty minutes past his paid-for time. Marita—" the madam pauses to cross herself "—was just like this. The boy was laying on the bed, like I say, passed out drunk and snoring."

"And so you sent Manuel to find me," Héctor says, feeling a headache coming on and squeezing the bridge of his nose. Manuel had found Héctor easily enough. The madam's errand boy put the arm on him in the Pale Fire Cantina, just a few blocks from his house in La Mesillia.

The madam squeezes Héctor's arm. She says, "Your ... the stories about you and what you do and what you write about ... well, I knew you could help me, Héctor, like nobody else can. We go back. And the boy, his family, is well known. And this other man, Stephen Walker, who is running for mayor, he's a moral crusader, yes? He's already trying to shut down operators like me. This killing in my house by this boy, well, you know what will happen, yes?"

Héctor nods. Walker is a bible-thumping madman and hypocrite of heroic proportions. A scripture-quoting politician and leading light of the Catholic Church.

But Héctor Lassiter, "poet of the gutters, borderlands and bawdy houses," as Anthony Boucher has described him, moves in twilight circles. The better to gather source material. Héctor has heard the stories of Walker's border crossings, tales of the politician's visits to Juarez brothels that offer children to rich pervert gringos. The couple of times Héctor met Walker, the politician stunk of breath mints, as if they could mask the smell of fifty-five years of gin-swilling.

And the passed-out boy in the other room? He is Joseph Newton, son of Evan Newton, New Mexico oil tycoon. Héctor smiles crookedly, thinking to himself, *Quite a cast of characters*.

The fat old madam wrings her pudgy hands, her eyes searching Héctor's face. "I don't know what I can offer you to make you help me with this mess."

But he's between books, going through a rare dry spell, right when he owes a short story to *Stag*. Lucky for him, life has imitated art has imitated life for so long that he increasingly confuses his memories for his stories. And Héctor knows his own carnal needs all too well. He has a too-firm and sad handle on his own animal impulses and desires.

So he says, "How about house credit through the New Year?" In two days, it will be Cinco de Mayo. Eight months of gratis lays and jaw-jobs seems just compensation for the gig.

The brothel matron nods vigorously. "Done. What should we do now?"

Héctor grinds out his cigarette on the bottom of his boot and tosses the stub aside. "Get a big rug or something we can roll poor Marita up in." As an afterthought, he asks, "She got family around here?"

The oldest whore shakes her head. "No, not here. They're on the other side. Somewhere in the Yucatan."

Héctor nods. Somehow that makes it a little easier to take liberties with the girl's already decimated reputation. It's pretty tough to libel the dead. "While you do that," Héctor says, "have Manuel pull my car around. It's the blue Chevy convertible parked out back."

The other whores help roll their fallen sister in the tasseled rug, and Héctor shoulders the load. He gently lays Marita out in the trunk of the Chevy and softly shuts the lid. *Poor little bitch. Dead and still has a busy night ahead of her.*

"What else?" the big madam asks, fanning herself more vigorously in the sultry New Mexico night.

"Fetch me three bottles of whatever young Joe was drinking before he evidently decided to try and twist off our Marita's head."

The madam gestures at one of her girls—a topless and sullen white girl with bad teeth and a horse face—who trudges inside to do her madam's bidding. Héctor shakes his head. If he ever uses of any of this, he's going to have to write about a whore prettier than that. As is, she's detracting from the scenery.

The wonting whore returns with the three bottles of tequila and Héctor stows them on the passenger seat. He instructs Manuel to squeeze into the back seat with the boy murderer.

Turning to the madam a last time, Héctor says, "I need to know you'll all never talk about this. Not you, and especially not your girls. I wasn't here tonight, right? Marita wasn't working here tonight, right? That boy never reached here tonight, right? This ever goes public, I tell the tale, got it?"

Madam Ruiz crosses herself. "You have my word."

Héctor doesn't want to dwell on what his pledge might or might not be worth.

"Alright then," he says. "Just threaten your girls within an inch of their lives if they ever let slip any of this."

Then he slides behind the wheel and sets off for the better side of town.

* * *

Manuel asks, "What first? Drop Joe off at home?"

Héctor shakes his head. "No way. I love my car and it's still eighty degrees in the dark. Poor Marita won't keep." Héctor passes a bottle of tequila over his shoulder to Manuel. "See if you can get some more of this into Joe ... as much as you can."

Manuel shakes his head. "I get it," he says, "keep him drunk and passed out, *si*, Mr. Lassiter?"

Actually, Héctor is shooting for a darker urge. But for now Héctor says, "Sure."

He palms the wheel, drifting into a filling station lot and next to a phone booth. He climbs out, pulling some change from his pants pocket and then pulling out and shaking loose his display handkerchief. He slips a dime between his own teeth and bites down on it. Talking through those clenched and blocked teeth will change the cadence and tone of his voice, and the layers of hand-kerchief over the receiver will do more of the same. The other coins go into the phone.

A presumptive mayor, Stephen Walker, answers.

Héctor says, "This is the call you've feared, asshole. And don't hang up. I have pictures of your fucking kids."

Silence.

"Is your family home?"

"No."

"Good," Héctor says. "Get in your car. Drive to where I am ... just across the bridge at Rosie's. I'll be the gringo with the camera. And a stack of photos. And, yes, the negatives, too. And here's the good news: I'm cheap. Five thousand dollars, and it all goes away."

Héctor hangs up without waiting for an answer. He slides back behind the wheel and cracks the seal on a bottle of tequila and takes a deep swig. He's committed now, and never was one to start something and not carry it to its end, even if it proves not to be a keeper.

There aren't many roads in La Mesillia. Stephen Walker has to drive by this parking lot to make his border crossing. Walker drives a brand-new black Cadillac with big red-white-and-blue campaign signs mounted on either side. Less than five minutes later, the favorite to be the town's next mayor goes rolling by in his impossible-to-miss Caddy billboard.

Héctor gets his Chevy in gear and drives in the opposite direction to Walker's house. Manuel starts looking nervous as they roll up before the big house. Héctor hands him the open bottle of tequila and says, "Finish her off."

While Manuel goes at the bottle, Héctor slides out of his car and scopes the Walker house. The front door looks impregnable, so he walks around back and finds a screen door. He slips out a library card and wedges it in the wide crack and easily pops the catch-and-eye hook securing the rickety door.

Then he goes back around the house and helps Manuel pull

Marita's body from the trunk. Huffing, they lug the carpet and its contents inside, up the stairs, and roll the dead prostitute's nude body onto the potential mayor's bed.

Manuel rolls the carpet up again and heads back to the Chevy as Héctor slips another dime between his teeth and, using the handkerchief again, scoops up the mayor's phone and dials the police. Disgusted to have to wait through nine rings, he finally gets a cop and lays out his confession as Stephen Walker. He goes for something breathless and psychotic, really getting into it. As Walker, he lays out plans to disappear, and says he hopes the cops will make his wife and kids understand.

Pleased, Héctor hangs up the phone, trots down the steps and runs to his Chevy. The night is full of sirens. It's a heady thing, shaping the face of a city to your own designs.

Manuel, now in the front seat next to Héctor, flying on tequila, says dreamily, "What now, *jefe*?"

Héctor takes the empty bottle and says, "I have a few more calls to make."

***

There are four significant whorehouses in La Mesillia. Héctor knows——and is known in——all of them. He makes inquiries and finds that his worst suspicions about the young Joe Newton are on target. To Héctor, a near-cherry boy doesn't just get drunk and get off and then decide to break a woman's neck and sleep it off.

He drops dimes and quickly learns at least five local working girls have died just as Marita has. The girls were presumably killed by Joseph Newton. In most cases, the boy's father paid money to cover up Joe's crimes. In a couple of cases, the madams or the pimps, in the manner of Madam Ruiz, elected to undertake their own cover-ups.

Héctor hangs up the phone and slides back behind the wheel. Manuel has drunk himself unconscious. His head is pressed to the passenger's side door and he's snoring, a drool-trail sliding down toward his collar. But it's just as well.

He drives out of town and into the desert, far enough away to avoid anyone, but close enough to be within plausible walking distance of town. From years of scratching out crime stories, Héctor has learned this: not everything can be told as it truly was. Some things are too true to be good when boiled down to prose.

With his handkerchief, Héctor wipes down the three bottles of tequila, and then presses each one several times into still-unconscious Joe Newton's hand. He hauls the boy out into the desert scrub and drops him across an anthill. Grasping their necks with the handkerchief, he arranges the three tequila bottles around the snoring boy.

According to whoever finds him, Joe got legless drunk, went off his head and wandered off into the desert night to his doom. It's predicted to drop down into the twenties by midnight. There is already a fierce west-to-east wind. All the liquor ... the ants ... the rattlesnakes and scorpions and the cold ... one or all of them will have their way with Joe, Héctor figures. If not, there'll be another killer, and maybe he'll yield another story. But no more working girls will fall prey to Joe's strangling hands. Not on Héctor's watch.

He breaks off a branch of scrub oak and wipes away the heel marks from Joe's body back to the Chevy from which he was dragged. Driving back to the Ruiz whorehouse, he surveys the night. There are plenty of potential pitfalls. What if Joe has told someone where he was bound this night? What if Joe has paid for Marita's favors before and told someone of those times? If so, Joe and Marita dying on the same night could raise serious questions, even in the minds of the lackluster local law.

Héctor rolls down the window and runs his hand back through his graying-brown hair. Yes, there are holes in his plots that could spell trouble later. But this is just a first draft. He tells himself he'll fix it all later, if or when he ever gets around to putting it all down on paper.

***

By midnight, Héctor is stretched out between two big-breasted blonds when the madam slides through the door without knocking, a fresh bottle of tequila and some ham sandwiches wrapped in wax paper arranged on the tray in her hands.

"They've arrested Stephen Walker for murder," she says. "It's on the radio. Even if it never sticks, he'll never be mayor now."

Héctor nods, trying to slide an arm out from behind one of the whore's heads in order to take the tray from madam Ruiz.

She smiles and asks, "Think you'll ever write about this, Héctor?"

He smiles back and talks with his mouth full. "Hard to say, honey. Sometimes they live better than they read."

The Alcoholic Monkey Who Took Over My Mind and Turned Me Into a Cold-Blooded Killer

BY JEFFREY DINSMORE

"Let me be straight, pal," the pet store owner said. "You don't want this monkey. This isn't an ordinary, 'put a clown outfit on me and watch me juggle' kinda monkey. This monkey is an alcoholic. He will drink you out of house and home, and he will ruin your life."

"Not having it," I replied. "That thing's fucking cute, and I'm taking it home with me. Wrap it up."

"But ..." the pet store owner began.

"WRAP UP THE FUCKING MONKEY!"

Hands shaking, the pet store owner cut a swath of wrapping paper and encased the docile beast inside. He handed the monkey to me.

"Where's the fucking bow, you cheap bastard?" I asked.

The pet store owner started to shake his head 'no' until he saw the cold-blooded look in my eyes. This thing was a present, and I wasn't leaving without a pretty pink bow on top.

When I got home that night, Jeannie was masturbating to *Roadhouse*. I tossed the package at her while she was mid-stroke.

"What's this?" she asked.

"Open it."

She undid the wrapping paper and squealed with delight. The monkey looked up at her with a grin.

"Oh, Jack, it's beautiful!" she said, tears welling up in her eyes.

"Glad you like it, babe," I said. "Now gimme that fucking thing. We got some drinking to do."

Three hours later, the monkey and I were sprawled out on the kitchen floor, soaked with piss and gin.

"Goddamn, monkey, that guy wasn't kidding," I said. "You sure can drink."

"Ook ook," the monkey said.

"Lemme just stand up here ..." I started to raise myself from the linoleum, but didn't get too far before collapsing back into a heap. The monkey laughed.

"Shut up, you fucking nitwit!" I shouted at him.

He kept laughing.

"You want me to kill someone, is that what you want?"

He kept laughing.

"All right, monkey," I said. "If it'll stop you from laughing, I'll kill someone. Jump on my shoulder. Let's go slaughtering."

The monkey and I snuck into my neighbor's house and killed him and his wife in their bedroom. I didn't feel good about it, but they were assholes, so good riddance. That guy borrowed my grouter once and when he returned it, it was all covered in chocolate.

The next morning, Jeannie woke me up with a shake.

"I just have one question for you," she said. "Did you and that monkey kill the neighbors last night?"

I searched my brain, but no memories were coming back to me.

"I doubt it," I said.

She breathed a sigh of relief. "When the cops showed up this morning and told me that their bed sheets were covered with monkey fur, I jumped to conclusions. I will never doubt you again."

"Damn right, babe," I said. "Now let's get it on."

She licked my anus and I spooged all over her face. Afterwards, the monkey walked in, carrying a beer.

"Damn, monkey, you're getting started early," I said.

"Ook ook," he confirmed.

"Hey honey, can I take the monkey with me today?" Jeannie asked. "I've got to do some shopping, and I was thinking he might want to go."

The monkey nodded his head.

Hours later, Jeannie and the monkey came back to find me masturbating to *Roadhouse*. The monkey cracked open a beer and handed me the rest of the six pack.

"Did you get any Cheetos?" I asked Jeannie.

"I didn't have enough money," she said. "The monkey bought too much alcohol."

I looked down at the little fucker. He was grinning like the cat that ate the canary.

"Well, I knew what I was getting into," I said to him.

I didn't like the look he gave me.

"Babe," I said, "I think the monkey wants me to kill again."

Jeannie was in the kitchen, putting away the alcohol.

"Dammit, Jack!" she said. "I thought you told me you didn't kill the neighbors!"

"Well, I forgot," I said sheepishly.

"This goddamn monkey is tearing us apart!" she screamed.

After I killed Jeannie, me and the monkey went out into town to get some more drinks and murder some more people. At the bar, the monkey's eyes landed on a sweet little co-ed with an enormous fat ass. I'm pretty sure he wanted me to nail her and then leave her body in a ditch. So, I started talking to her.

"What's your major?" I asked.

"Monkey studies," she said. "That's a cute monkey."

"You're goddamn right," I said. "You wanna get out of this shit-hole?"

"I thought you'd never ask," she answered.

We went back to her dorm room and she stripped the panties off her fat ass. The monkey jumped on her back and played her ass cheeks like bongos. She giggled.

"Ook, ook," she said, and the monkey stopped.

"Say, that's pretty good, babe," I said. "Do you speak monkey?"

"Ook, ook," she said, and the monkey did a little pirouette.

"Maybe I should give him to you," I said. "I have no idea how to control this goddamn thing."

"Ook, ook," she said, and the monkey lunged for my throat.

"Say, what's the big deal?" I choked out.

"Just kidding," she said, and the monkey stopped choking me. "You wanna get it on?"

We fucked each other until our genitals were a bloody mess. Afterwards, she suggested we watch *Roadhouse*. Then there was a knock on the door.

"Open up, it's the police!"

"Shit," I said. "I gotta be honest with you, babe, I've killed a couple people. I was gonna kill you, too, but then you had such a way with the monkey, I just couldn't bring myself to do it."

She smiled.

"Ook, ook."

The monkey opened the door and let the cops in. They were going to take me to jail, but that fucking monkey got them so drunk they forgot why they were there. The co-ed fucked us all bloody, and then we all went to the student union to play some pool.

"I'll tell you what," I said, knocking in the 8 ball to end the game. "This has been a pretty good day."

The cops laughed, and the co-ed laughed, and all the people in the world laughed, except for the monkey. He knew we'd kill again.

The monkey was right, to some extent. We ran over a baby in the road a few weeks later in Duluth. After that, we got so shit-faced that I don't even remember what happened.

The French Clock

BY JEFFREY KUCZMARSKI

Mr. Bard remembered how it started, how raindrops struck the windows of the squat brick house like fists and how Ruben, his one-eyed black lab, howled once before he died as if he'd seen a glimpse of doggie hell, and the neighbor's cat was waiting, claws drawn. Before the rap on his door came, he examined the beautiful French clock he'd purchased at an antique store in Paris; its only flaw was a dark scorch mark, an empty place near a tangle of intricately carved vines. The dealer with whom he worked felt sure the spot once contained a wood sprite or similar creature in keeping with the woodland theme. One other unusual detail that caught his eye was a worn silver ring with a stone he couldn't identify; it was set above the black, tarnished space. Once he saw the clock, he could think of nothing else. He had to possess it.

Mr. Bard was about to wind the clock when the lights went out without the customary decency of even a flicker or two, and the silver tea kettle on the iron stove began to scream its high-pitched, I'm-being-chased-by-a-serial-killer scream. His heart beat fast from the whiskey or the lack of a refill. Fortunately, he had a flashlight with dead batteries, no matches, and candles that smelled of cin-namon. The Boy Scouts taught him well; even though he'd dropped out in the second grade, he was always prepared. He felt his way through the darkness and managed to slip in the last pool of drool Ruben ever drooled and come down on his hindquarters with a thump. He saw falling stars blaze through the room, illuminating the darkness. His head did a wino's walk as he stood up and saun-tered forward, blind as a newborn pup. The thought of disposing of man's best friend didn't help, nor did the resounding *thud-thud* of someone knocking on the front door.

"You must be Mr. Bard?" asked a beautiful woman with raven eyes, handing him a shovel with her gloved hand. She smelled like a greenhouse.

"Mr. James Finneaus Bard," he said, shaking her hand tenta-tively. "And who may I ask are you, and what are you doing at my door with a shovel on this rainiest, darkest, and most macabre of nights?"

"My name is Ms. Prophecy Jones. Your dog died, fleas are bit-ing you, and I need to tell you a story. I see you have purchased my clock."

"Your clock? I'm not sure I understand. I paid for this clock. I can show you the receipt if you like."

"That is not necessary, Mr. Bard. I'll tell my story once you turn on the lights. Here, take these batteries for your flashlight and run to the basement fuse box and flip the switch."

In the light, Prophecy Jones was even more remarkable than she was in darkness. She seemed to blossom under the glow of the halogen bulbs. Her obsidian eyes caught the light and absorbed, compressed, and polished it until he nearly swooned from her sheer intensity and he either had to look away or be consumed. She was a large, middle-aged woman who was comfortable in her largeness. As she began speaking, her words had a hypnotic charm that tore away any of his reservations and drew him in like a satellite entering a planet's orbit.

She did not waste words, and this was the story that unfolded from her lips:

"My story starts five-hundred years ago at Armand's, the watchmaker's shop in Paris on the *Rue de Temps*. Armand was constructing a most beautiful clock for the Duke de la Mort, who made an impossible demand of the poor overworked and underpaid clockmaker. The Duke commanded a clock that never needed winding and always kept perfect time. The clock was to stand nine-feet tall and be made of the finest cedar and oak. The inner gears were to be of the strongest and purest silver and gold to prevent wear. The face was to be made of solid jade with diamonds that would make emperors jealous, marking the hours. The two hands were to be crafted from the finest Baltic blood amber ever to be found in Latvia. Armand had worked for a year-and-a-half straight and had just begun to finish the required ivory inlay on the mahogany doors. He wept when he set the gears in motion and saw the amber hands move like perfectly choreographed dancers across the delicate jade face. This was the best work of his life and he knew it.

"'So, it is finally finished,' he said to the cobwebs in the corners of his little shop. He had worked on the problem of perpetual motion for a year and discovered a brilliant, yet simple, solution: sunlight. Of course, perpetual motion was impossible, so the key to the problem was to fool the Duke de la Mort into believing that the clock ran perpetually. To achieve this illusion, Armand had cleverly persuaded the Duke to allow him to place the clock in the Duke's castle upon its completion. Armand carved tiny slits in the back of the clock and hid them among the inlay work of the back of the clock and placed a magnifying lens inside the clock's case to intensify the sun's rays. He then made hundreds of tiny coils of the finest gold and placed them where they would absorb the most sun and connected them to a winding mechanism. During the day, the coils would expand in the heat enough to drop a series of brass weights that would spin gears that wound the clock. At dusk, the reverse occurred as the sun's rays dissipated the coils, which tightened in the cold, causing the metal weights to be retracted, winding the clock. Armand even accounted for cloudy days. The clock only had to be wound every twelve days.

"The Duke de la Mort was a most powerful and imposing man. He had a reputation as the cruelest man in all of France. He once tarred and feathered a cook for failing to pluck all of the feathers from a goose. The Duke then had the cook completely cleaned of tar and feathers, cooked in his own famous orange sauce, and fed to the Duke's favorite hounds. The Duke was also a master of dark and binding magic, and was often seen levitating in the moonlight and entertaining evil spirits.

"Clearly, the Duke was not a man to be refused. A long trail of missing persons dead-ended at his palace and, from time to time, a traveler late upon the road told tavern tales of hearing screams from within that tore the night's peace. Armand had justifiable misgivings when the Duke's request was delivered, but what could he do but accept the commission and agree to build the clock?"

Enmeshed in the images Prophecy had created, her voice painting syllables like dense oils on canvas, a moment passed before Mr. Bard realized she had stopped speaking.

"May I have a glass of that excellent sherry you keep in your sideboard?"

Amazed at the intimacy of her knowledge, Mr. Bard rose and crossed the threadbare rug.

Ruben had elected to breathe his last breath directly in front of the long cabinet, completely blocking both doors. Bard's guest watched with her raven eyes as he struggled to shift the stiffening corpse. As cooperative in death as the dog was in life, this process took much longer and looked more foolish than he cared for. Still on his knees, Bard rummaged out the decanter and located two mismatched glasses, one of which contained a long-dead moth. He dumped out the bug and uncorked the sherry. Instantly, the room filled with the scent of wood smoke and sun-warmed cherries. He poured precisely two inches of blood garnet liquor into each glass, then turned.

He had not heard her rise, and she had crossed the room so soundlessly that he almost dropped the sherry when he became aware of her presence. He could smell her scent of deep places and secrets as she lifted a glass from his fingers. She sniffed delicately, catlike, too small a movement for such a large woman.

"Ah, now that's lovely," she said. She took a long sip and resumed her tale.

"Now that Armand's work was finished after nearly two years, he realized that he had fallen in love with his creation. Tenderly, he put his fingers against the wood, felt the grain, and swelled with pride. But then his hand felt an empty spot hidden among the intricate jeweled vines and flowers right above the hand of a nymph. The clockmaker gasped, stepping back. He could leave it and no one would know but him. Oh, but how that thought burned in his mind! It would never do to leave the work unfinished. He searched his workshop floor for one misplaced gem to fill the void, but there were none to be found. All of them had been used. It was then that he remembered the ring.

"A poor Paris watchmaker did not usually possess treasures himself, but Armand owned one precious object: his grandmother's ring. Quickly, he opened a small drawer concealed underneath his workbench and fumbled among the cobwebs for the box. He found it, slid it out, and unhooked the brass catch. At first glance, the thin silver band was an unremarkable piece, but on further study it was set with a stone like no other. He remembered watching the ring on his grandmother's hand, how when they chatted and laughed, it seemed to glow as if absorbing the energy of the happy moment for some later purpose. Even now he was unable to determine its exact color; it was the purest forest green one moment, a deep-sea indigo the next. His grandmother told him it was very old and that it had the power to grant him one wish, but she died before she could tell him how to use it.

"Armand placed the ring with infinite care directly above the nymph's outstretched hand and then collapsed in an exhausted heap at the foot of the clock.

"He awoke the next day to the sound of the Duke's guards banging on the door. The guards wrapped the clock and hefted it onto the cart. They threw the clockmaker in like a sack of potatoes and hurried to deliver the prize to their master.

"The clock was positioned directly in front of the large window in the Duke's central hall. As the Duke watched, Armand wound the clock, setting the gears in their 'perpetual motion.' When this was done, Armand knew the time he dreaded had come. He would have to part with his masterpiece. He gazed one final time upon the clock's beautiful face, and his eyes sought the ring with its magical jewel hidden among the vines. He wept with joy. He was so absorbed by his creation that he did not hear the Duke draw his blade as he approach him from behind. He did not feel the wound itself but the warmth of his own blood running like a river down his neck and arms. As he fell to the floor dying, the jewel burned as red as Armand's blood, and he commanded that the nymph come to life and protect the clock. And so, at that moment the ring glowed and shot flame like a miniature sun, momentarily blinding everyone in the room, and then it went out like a candle snuffed by a high wind; its power transferred to the nymph, who made a shrieking sound that caused everyone to turn and gasp with horror as she took full shape, an awful scowl branded on her face as she endured the pain of birth.

"The nymph's vengeance was swift and horrible. She turned the guards into sour cherry trees that would know no peace from birds, insects, or the hands of greedy men. She morphed the Duke's guests into truffles and let pigs free from their pens. She filled the moat with vines and turned the brick floor into dirt and everything else in the room, except the clock, grew a layer of mold and had the reek of decay. She reserved her full fury for the Duke, whom she transformed into a giant snail, which she imbued with regenerative powers so she could hack him to pieces over and over for centuries without ever dealing a fatal blow," finished Ms. Jones.

Mr. Bard swallowed and nervously squirmed in his chair, then said, "That's a remarkable story. I'll be sure to take extra, extra care."

"Excellent. Now, you must be famished? How about an escargot and mushroom pie before you bury that dog under one of those cherry trees?" she asked, but didn't wait for a response. Instead, she rose, pulled a stained cleaver from the depths of her handbag, and followed the slime trail outside to the enormous snail grazing on the lawn. As she swung the blade over her head and down, she grinned, revealing row upon row of teeth and a tongue as black and inescapable as a pit of tar.

Mr. Bard, with no small effort, pulled his eyes away and told himself not to worry.

***

"Finish your plate dear, don't be rude."

"I can't. The smell is so musty and so, so, sweet."

"Well, put some more salt on it. Drink some wine."

"I can't, every day it's the same meal, the same story, like the hours of the day, like the chiming of that goddamn clock. I wish I had never set eyes on it," said Bard as he jumped to his feet and ran out of the house to the shed. There he looked wildly around for it, sweat soaking his shirt as he tossed objects out of his path. "Where is it?" he muttered as panic put on a chokehold that caused him to breath in short, explosive bursts. "I saw it only yesterday. Think, think," he said as he darted this way and that in the dim light. Near collapse, he stubbed his toe on something. He hopped on one foot and looked down, and there it was: the sledgehammer. He picked it up, grinned and backtracked.

She was waiting for him but wasn't prepared for the ferocity of his charge.

"The train is coming through; get your ticket out or get off," he said and swung the hammer into her chest as she leapt at him. She flew backward and landed hard. He kept moving and made a beeline for the clock.

"What do you think you're doing?" she asked a few moments later.

"Oh, you'll see, and better yet, you'll hear." He raised the hammer high over his head and took a mighty swing. Wood splinters flew through the air.

"Now, why would you do that? I thought you would last longer than the others, that you were stronger. I guess I was wrong." Jones sliced the cleaver into his side just as he stood poised to take another swing.

Bard dropped the hammer and clutched the handle of the

blade. He pulled it out, took in as much air as he could, turned, and stabbed at the face of the clock where the ring sat. Blood dripped onto the floor. He cut deeper.

Jones stood stunned. He had more fight in him than she knew. He would need to be punished and punished severely.

"No, no! I won't let you spoil everything!" Jones lunged, stuck her hand in the wound in his side, and squeezed.

Bard screamed, but was undeterred. He dug the knife deeper into the wood and pried until the ring was free.

Now, it was Jones's turn to scream as the hands of the clock came to a stop, and Bard lodged the knife to the hilt in her throat. She fell to the floor, flopped like a fish without air, and went still.

Bard collapsed, too. And as he died, he looked up at the clock. Its architecture sagged as if worm-eaten, and it was blackened, as if it had narrowly escaped a tremendous fire.

Bard grinned weakly.

He had done it.

But then he heard a faint noise, a chime, followed by another and another until the hour sounded and his body was cold upon the floor.

The Candy Man

BY MATTHEW FRIES

I found out some little prick at the Meister warehouse up off County Road 9 was ripping off one of my machines. That's how it started. Every week I'd drive up there to collect my sugar and find the machine was light. In my line of work, you just can't let that slide.

I noticed some scratches on the side of the machine. They were digging in through the door with a bent-up clothes hanger. It was one of the new machines, too. I paid big dough for it. A Taylor 3000, supposedly impenetrable.

The vending machine was in a small lunchroom—about four tables. I filled it every other Friday, and the kids knew my schedule. So, I mixed it up a bit to throw them off. I drove up there in the van on a Thursday at about 9:00 p.m., when the afternoon shift went on break (I figured it was the kids on the afternoon shift because there were too many bosses around during the day for them to get away with shit like that). I sat in the van behind the warehouse and waited. I could see through the warehouse bay door. The workers all left the line where they sorted packages for a large shipping company. I got out of the van and went into the warehouse. I waited around the corner of the lunchroom. I could hear them in there.

"Get the coat hanger," I heard one of them say.

I could hear the coat hanger scratching the side of the machine. They might as well have been digging at my heart.

They were laughing. "Get me a Big Turk," the one kid said.

Little fucks.

I came around the corner and stood in the doorway. They scattered to the corners. I went after the kid with the bent-up coat hanger. He tried to whip me in the leg with it, but I slapped him hard in the face. Slapping people scares the hell out of them. I learned that in the pen. He dropped the coat hanger. The others made for the door. Fine. I let them go. I only needed one of the little bastards to set an example.

I slapped him again. He started to cry. Didn't mean nothing to me.

"You got a sweet tooth?" I asked him.

"I wasn't doing nothing, dude."

I slugged him in the gut. I figured him to be about eighteen, with a cheese-eating moustache and pants that were about thirteen sizes too big for him. He had a giant fake diamond earring in his ear and a gold chain with a hubcap pendant. He looked tough, but I could tell he'd never really had a real ass-kicking before. Not like the one he was about to get. He folded over, then groaned and melted to the floor.

I slapped the top of his head and gave him a quick upper-cut to the nose. Thought I heard something snap.

He fell back onto the concrete floor.

"You musta took me for thirty bucks by now, you little shit," I growled.

"C'mon, guy. What the fuck's your problem? It's only a candy bar!"

He was on his back. Blood was running out his nose and over his cheeks. Blood and little crybaby tears.

"I'm gonna knock that sweet tooth right outta yer head," I said. "Sit up, pussy."

He did.

"Empty your pockets."

He dug in his pockets and threw his keys and a couple twenties on the floor.

"That ain't enough," I told him. "Where's the wallet?"

He clammed up.

"Where's your damn wallet, boy? I'm sick of you little turds ripping me off. Where's your wallet?"

"I don't carry one. That's all I got, mister," he spat through the blood running over his lips.

"Gimme the chain."

"Fuck you!" he spat again. "My mom gave it to me," he said, now crawling under a table toward the corner.

I caught him by the pants, pulled him back out, and bent down over him, feeding his face with a flurry of hard shots—just enough to straighten him up and make him do the right thing without knocking the little bastard out. I got his blood all over me.

He was groggy but still together. I wanted him to see this. I ripped the chain off his neck and picked up the twenties from the floor. "You fuck with my machine again," I said, "or you mouth off to the pigs about this, and I'll be back here with a lead pipe."

"My mom's boyfriend is gonna kill you, you piece of shit."

"Fine," I said. "Long as he doesn't steal from me." I left him there to pull himself together before the ambulance came for him.

I was feeling pretty high on myself as I walked to the van.

Nothing like a good fight. I sang my song … "The Candy Man can 'cause he mixes it with love and makes the world taste good …" and threw the chain into the woods. Wasn't worth shit. Nothing but goddamned cheap, gold paint.

***

I've always been on the nut. That's just it. No jobs in this area, no money to move, hard living. Then, in my early twenties, I did a nickel for a break and enter I had very little to do with. I was the wheel man. A couple other guys done the real robbing. My third year in the pen, my old man, my only family, was blown up in an explosion at the rendering plant where he worked. Hell of a way to go. He left me the trailer and a bit of insurance money in his will. Woulda been more insurance dough, but the cocksucking insurance company said that the old boy was three sheets to the wind when he blew up. Said he caused that explosion himself. Said I was "lucky" to get what I was getting. Hell of a way to put it.

I took the money and invested it in vending machines. A guy in prison told me a man could make up to a grand a week if he had the stake to invest. Cons are so full of shit. I barely made enough sugar most times to pay for the trailer park fees, barely had enough to eat. Spent half my life driving the county stocking the vending machines, looking for new clients, living off bags of chips and pop, eating my inventory and getting ripped off. A man gets sick of being played for a sucker. Starts to get ornery. That was me.

So, it was about a week after I beat and robbed the kid at the warehouse when I was out making my rounds on my Dickie Dee ice cream cart. I never made any money hocking ice cream to house wives and their little brats. It was chump change, even if you short-changed the rubes or picked their pockets. There's no money in ice cream; it was just a cover for my other business. You see, the real money was in the park, selling dime bags of grass to high school kids. My clientele were a bunch of pizza-faced little shits, but their money was as good as anybody else's.

It was a fairly nice, sunny day, and I was admiring the tits and ass of a young blonde teenager when I noticed the local constabulary approaching me. Lem Lowry. I had known Lem since I was a kid. Went to school with him. I had heard that he was the one who sent me up the river on that B and E. Ratted me out to get a job on the police force. Now the sonofabitch had a license to steal. I hated him, but what was I gonna do? He was the boss in these parts.

So, Lem came up to the park. The kids I sold grass to scattered. I couldn't run unless I ditched my cart. It was too heavy to move quickly, so I was on the hook for whatever was about to go down. Fuck it. What was he gonna do? Bust me for a couple dime bags of grass? Wasn't worth his time.

Lem walked slowly towards me in his brown Sheriff's uniform, checking the sky as he walked.

"Looks like it might rain, Candy Man," Lem said as he came up on me.

"What can I do ya' for, Lem?" I asked.

"Lemme see … what you got here? How's them Astro Bars?"

"Outta this world. Just like the sign says," I told him.

"I think I'll skip on the ice cream today. Hook a brother up with some tea."

"Tea? You see any boiling water around here?"

"Don't give me that shit," he said. "You know damn well what I'm talkin' about."

"Tea? I ain't gettin' you."

"Reefer. Grass, man. Some Mary Jane."

"Mary Jane! Reefer? Shit, man. Tea? Last time I checked it

wasn't 1967."

"Guess I'm a little square," Lem said. "Nevermind, then." He paused for a second, staring at the sky. Then he looked at me with his steel grey eyes. Meaner than cat piss. Whatever Lem wanted, he meant business. I knew he wasn't looking to bust me for the dime bags of pot, though. He never had before.

"So, you were out at the Meister warehouse the other day?"

"Last week," I said. "I was restocking the Taylor I got out there."

"Some kid got the shit kicked out of him. Know anything about it?"

"Don't know nothing about it, Lem."

"Sure you do, Candy Man. At least gimme a hug if you're gonna fuck me. Else I'll cry rape."

I didn't answer him.

"I know what happened. You think I'm stupid?"

My guess was he wanted an answer. "No," I said. The only answer fit for a guy like him.

"Just between you and me, the kid's a little bastard. He needed a beating like that. Probably straighten him right up. Problem is, you see, his mother is my maid. And she's been, let's just say, 'cleaning my pipe' lately."

I suddenly understood what the kid meant when he said, "My mom's boyfriend's gonna kill you."

"Classy, Lem," I said, "You're fucking your maid."

I had forgotten who I was talking to. Lem gave me a whack. I fell over backwards, the Dickie Dee cart falling on top of me. Nearly broke my leg. Ice cream bars and dime bags of weed spilled out all over the grass. I came to a couple seconds afterward, too stunned to even notice the throbbing pain that I would soon feel in my right eye.

Lem was beside me, resting on his haunches, staring up at the sky. A little outburst of violence like that ruffled him no more than a gentle breeze through his hair.

"I want you to do me a favor, Candy," he said, finally looking me in the eye.

I kept quiet.

"Remember my brother, William?"

"Fuck William!" I said.

"Yeah, that's the guy," Lem said. "He's going through a bad spell. Financially, that is. He needs a place to live. He's a musician. He's got a big grant from the government coming in this summer. Lotta dough. He should be outta your hair by then. I'll make sure of it."

"Why don't you look after him?" I argued. "I ain't gonna babysit that idiot! He's *your* brother."

"I can't stand him," Lem told me.

"Fuck you, Lem," I said with as much venom as I could muster.

"Well, well, well. Candy Man, the big baller. Finally gets enough guts to stand up for himself. A man with priors could get into a lot of trouble for kicking the shit out of a minor. That kid you beat up was only sixteen. Last time I checked, assault on a minor carried a ten-year sentence. You could be on ice until you're forty-three."

"Fuck," I moaned.

"William will be out to your place on Tuesday. We got us a relationship here, Candy." Lem reached into the grass by my head. I was sure I was gonna get it again. I braced myself for another ass-kicking.

Lem picked up a dime bag of weed and held it up for me to see. "Got any rolling papers?" he asked.

I felt like I was frozen all the way through.

"Okay," Lem said, standing up and walking away, taking the

weed with him.

I watched him go as I sat up. I reached out and grabbed a cold Fudgeo bar to put over my now-throbbing eye. Falling back on the grass, I said to myself, "Fucking brother. How bad could it be?"

***

Lem's fucking brother went two months without a shower. Two months! He was moldy. That ain't no lie.

William got up every day at noon. He would open his bedroom door and, still in his underwear, drag his fat ass to the bathroom for his morning turd. It would take a couple of seconds before the reek of his bedroom would follow him out the door. It made me gag. Then he would shit and brush his teeth, and the smell of the turd mixed with the toothpaste smell and the B.O. It made me so mad. And William didn't give a goddamn lick what anybody else thought, as if they were too low to have any opinions at all.

It didn't take long for the stench to take over everything. The couch began to stink, the chairs began to stink. And I cleaned. I sure as hell did. I did my best to fight it. I went to the co-op store in town and the counter girl with the nice big tits gave me this shit called Febreeze, which didn't work for a damn. I went to the hippy store and bought some incense, but nothing could stop the bastard's stink. It was a rising tide, and the worse it got, the angrier I got. I was drowning in it. I hated his fucking guts. I dreamed of cutting his throat.

I told the sonofabitch to shower, and he laughed at me. He told me to go back in the can and talk to one of the government shrinks to see if he could cure me of my faggotry.

That's what he fucking said.

***

I had no choice but to move out to the shed where I stored my candy. I set up a cot and watched him from the window, getting madder and madder.

He'd get up at noon every day in my goddamn trailer, have his shit, then yawn and cough for an hour or so, recuperating from a night of sleeping. He'd eat Captain Crunch out of an old dog food bowl that he found in the cupboard and then finally pull a pair of grimy old jeans over his skid-marked underwear. Every day.

A man can get pretty fucking pissed off in two months.

I still had to use the bathroom in the trailer. My once-white hand towel that I kept in the bathroom was now yellowish-grey.

He lived in my trailer, and I watched him from my shed. At one o'clock every day he'd sit at his electronic keyboard, shirtless, and scratch his giant, greasy, bald spot with two fingers. Then he'd doze off with his chin in his chest, his long hair looking like strips of raw bacon trailing down his hairy back.

And the money. The government grants started coming in. Lem wasn't shitting me. William had the perfect scam going. He'd apply for government grants to make music. He watched television from *Oprah* at 4:00 p.m. until reruns of *Saturday Night Live* at 2:00 in the morning. But he did not make music. Ever. He just filled out the forms for grants and waited on the checks.

He got his girlfriend Velena to cash the checks for him because he was too lazy to leave the trailer park. The only thing he ever did, besides watch television, was run up a tab with the Italian bookies who were renting the Airstream across the street.

Velena did everything for him. She brought him his Kentucky Fried Chicken and Big Macs and Taco Bell, his Captain Crunch and milk, and the daily racing forms. Velena. I don't know how she hooked up with him, or why, but he landed her all the same. The only way I could figure it was that she was a musician. I had heard him tell her once that he was going to make her famous. I spent many nights lying awake, trying to figure out what kind of woman would put up with his stench just for the promise of fame. It seemed impossible.

And it got worse. I told Lem that William's money was coming in and that William had to go. Lem told me that William liked it there and was not going to leave. He said that if I tried to throw him out he would arrest me on some trumped-up charge or kill me and toss my body in Pike Lake. He came by every Friday to remind me of our deal. I had two options as far as I could see: hit the road and leave William with the trailer—my trailer, my inheritance, the only thing I had in the world—or kill him.

***

When the big grant came in from the Canadian Council (a twenty-thousand dollar check for producing his nonexistent composition, which the fucking moron cashed and then stashed in a sack beneath the sink), I decided I should probably kill him. And I wasn't the only one who was thinking about it, either.

One night, Velena came into my shed. I threw my cordless headphones around my neck and answered the door. She was crying. She had a black eye. I figured Stinky must have popped her one. She stood there in the door, sobbing, her back heaving, her breasts fat and jiggling with each breath. I could smell him on her.

"He hates me," she said.

"Why do you care?" I barked.

"He won't let me sing on his album."

"There is no fucking album, you dizzy bitch." I sat up on the edge of my little cot. "And why do you even care?" I shot. "Why? Is it that important to you?"

"You have to talk to him. You have to do something. He defiles me! Now he won't even let me play on the album. I hate him," she said. "I hate his rotten, stinking guts. He smells like a dead man."

"You're fucked, lady," I said. "You're fucked in the head. Nothing is worth putting up with that stench."

"Nothing?" she asked, staring at me like she wanted to rip a hole in my guts, her eyes red and swollen with rage and tears. She bounced like an angry child, which made her angry breasts heave and bounce even more. "Then why do you do it? Why do you let him push you out of your own home? Be a man. Stand up to them." She suddenly seemed to have an Eastern European harshness to her voice that I had never noticed before. It was damn sexy. "Kill him. Take the money," she said and stepped into the shed, slamming the little tin door shut behind her.

I fell back on the cot as she leapt on top of me. I could feel her flesh as she tore her clothes off. I struggled to get away from the stench of William, but she was filled with psychotic rage and strength.

"I hate him!" she kept saying as I finally managed to kick her off of me and roll her to the floor. She scratched at my face. I held her arms down. She kicked me off of her, and we rolled over again. She was on top with her shirt torn open. We were crushing all my bags of chips and all my chocolate bars. All the while I could smell him on her, but it didn't stop me. Kill him. Kill him. The crunching bags of chips. The smell of William made me fucking sick. It made me furious. It was not like we were making love; it was like we were fighting to the death. Making love. Making murder.

***

Not many people know this, but cordless headphones pick up cordless phone calls. If I tuned the frequency in right, I could listen to the phone calls of people throughout the trailer park, as long as they used a cordless phone. I found this out by accident one night and had a good laugh when I heard Mrs. Markdale talking to her sister about cheating on her impotent husband. I thought about blackmailing her, but she took off with her lover a day later. Since then I had always kept my ears peeled for any juicy tidbits and info I could use in the trailer park.

Across the road at the Elmvale Trailer Park, where the Italian bookies lived, William liked to gamble on the ponies. I didn't think much of it at first, but when he got the big check, I started thinking. If I was going to kill William and make off with his stash, I had to make sure that the bookies didn't get it all first.

My vending machines were all full, and the high school kids were getting into drugs like ecstasy and cocaine. Mary Jane was passé. Business was slow. I was stuck at home most of the time with William, thinking about ways I could kill him.

Then Lem came by on a Friday. I was halfway through a case of beer.

"How's life in the fast lane there, Big Baller?" Lem asked, getting out of the police cruiser in my driveway. He chuckled at my predicament.

It was raining slightly. "He's gonna give me the plague, Lem. He coughs constantly, but he doesn't smoke."

"It's a real bugger, eh?" Lem said. "He's incorrigible. Now you know why I couldn't have him living with me. You'll get used to it. Or at least you better get used to it before the winter." Lem laughed. "Or is this tin shed winterized? Where you gonna keep the snow blower?"

"What do you want, Lem?" I asked. "I already know the routine. You'll toss me in the cooler or off me if I don't keep looking after that retard in there. It's starting to sound half good, compared to what I'm living with now."

"Whatever," Lem said. "Did he get his grant? The music production one?"

"He did," I said. "He keeps sticking his fat, greasy head out the window and telling me that he's richer than a king."

"Good, good. Glad to see my fucking tax dollars go to a good place. So, has he bought anything?"

"Well, he ain't spent it on deodorant or soap. That's for damn sure," I told Lem. "All he does is give it to the bookies." I knew Lem wouldn't like that.

"Those fucking guidos? I thought I told them to cut that shit out!"

"They ain't scared of you, Lem. They ain't from around here."

"Don't I know it?" Lem said.

"It's a bugger," I said, pretending not to know what I was doing. But I could tell I was getting Lem pretty pissed.

"I'm gonna have to go have a talk with these guys," Lem said, turning.

I watched him walk across the road. The Italians were out barbecuing sardines, sitting on their picnic bench and drinking beer. I could smell the grilling fish.

Lem walked straight up to them and kicked the barbecue over. I could hear him shouting. "How much does he owe you?"

The Italians didn't answer. They didn't even move. You could tell that they were used to being hassled by the cops.

"You fucking rotten wop bastards, how much?" Lem socked

the one guy in the jaw and sent him flying off of the picnic table. He was lying on the ground twitching, out cold. Lem grabbed the other guy by the collar. "How much money is he in to you for, you fucking grease ball?"

"I don't even know who you're talking about, copper!"

"You see that trailer over there?" Lem pointed to my trailer. "That's my brother. Don't fuck with me. I told you guido shits before! Tell me how much he's in to you for. I'll make it easy on you," Lem slapped him in the face.

"Fuckin' country elbows worse than the city pigs," the Italian said.

"How much?"

"A couple G's. Nothing."

"Where is it? Give it to me!"

"Piss off, country dick."

Lem patted him gently on the cheek a couple of times. "I see you near that trailer, I'll have you back in the pen doing hard time again," he said. Lem stood and started to walk toward me. Then he did an about-face and kicked the bookie so hard in the face that I saw the fucker's tooth go flying from his head and land about ten yards away from him. He fell off the picnic table right on top of his buddy.

Lem turned, winked and smiled as he walked towards me. "You got off light, motherfucker," Lem shouted.

"This is fucking light?" the Italian raged from his mangled mouth. "Do you know who the fuck I am?" He seemed to be missing at least one of his front teeth. "Mario! Mario!" he was trying to shake his buddy awake.

Lem smirked and raised his arm out to shoot him the finger as he walked away, too goddamn ignorant to even turn and face him. The way I see it, if you are gonna do something like that to somebody, you should at least have enough goddamn class to turn and face him when you shoot him the finger. Damn right that Lem Lowry was a lowdown sonofabitch.

Lem got back in his car. "See you, Candy," he said as he peeled off.

The bookmaker was scowling over at me as Lem drove off. He stood up. His face was red as an apple, and it wasn't just from the blood that was pouring from his mouth.

I heard my trailer window open. "What's all the noise?" the stink of William drifted from the trailer out into the yard.

"Nothing," I told him.

"Well, keep it down out here. I'm trying to work," he barked and slammed the window.

Mario was now sitting up. The other guy was yelling at him in Italian and pointing toward my trailer. "Lo uccidere! O un uomo guasto!" Spitting gobs of blood.

I shut the door to the shed.

I watched the Italians through a crack in my shed door. They were stomping around furiously, kicking at the barbecue. The fatter of the two reached for the cordless telephone and went inside the trailer. I went for my headphones immediately.

"Frankie!"

Through some crackling static, I tuned it in a little better.

"What you calling here for? Siete pazzeschi?"

"I'm gonna kill somebody!"

"Passesco! You're on vacation. Who cares? Stay outta trouble 'til the heat's off."

"I'm gonna kill two people."

"Over the telephone you call me and you tell me you're gonna kill two people. Are you fucking stupid? What's wrong with your mouth? You're talking funny."

"I don't fucking care. This country cocksucking elbow and his fat fuck brother!"

"What did he do?"

"He knocked my fucking teeth out! The fat stinky fuck will die, too."

"He knocked out your teeth? What is this guy, a bull?"

"He's a fucking cop. I'm gonna kill his brother; then I'm gonna kill him."

"You gonna kill a cop's brother and a cop?"

"Orina su lui. The brother first, so the cop will suffer. Jesus Christ, Mother Mary, my goddamn face hurts like a bastard."

"Does the brother live alone?"

"No, there's some creep that lives in the shed. And a girl. Sometimes. Not too often anymore."

"Not too often? Well, you sure as fuck better find out. If you're gonna kill a cop's brother, you make sure there ain't no witnesses. And go to the hospital. Fix your teeth. You sound like a fucking fairy." Laughter.

"I'll whack every goddamn sonfoabitch in the fucking trailer park! The guy in the shed and the girl. Then I'll burn the place down. It'll look like an accident. Tonight!"

"Fuck, Nicky. Jesus Christ, you're gonna drive me mental. Moron! Well, go ahead then. What do I care? You draw any heat on me and you'll be a cement block. Why call here and tell me this any-way?"

"I needed your blessing."

"Go fuck yourself, Nicky. Do whatever the hell you want." He hung up.

This was it. It was perfect. Somebody was gonna kill William for me.

***

Unfortunately, they were planning on killing the Candy Man, too. A little wrinkle. I needed to figure out a way to stay alive myself and get the grant money beneath the sink.

I knew from the glow of the television at night that William had moved it into his bedroom, where he spent most of his time. I would wait until dark to make my first move.

I took an old cotton dress shirt—a clean one—and some lemon suckers. With the ass end of a hatchet, I smashed the lemon suckers into the shirt. Ground them in good. Then I tied the shirt around my face. The smell of sugary lemon was strong. I then took some tin snips and cut a hole in the back of my shed. I crawled out, leaving the door shut, so the Italian bookmakers would think I was still inside. I crawled around to the back of the trailer and went in through a window. It was dark

The stink. I could hear the television coming from William's room. I went in and stood in the closet by the door. My closet, with his coats in it. His reeking jean-jacket. I choked and gagged and tried to keep from puking. I tried to concentrate on the lemon suckers and sang to myself.

"The Candy Man can 'cause he mixes it with love and makes the world taste good."

I waited. I heard him grunting and laughing to himself at *The Late Show with David Letterman*. I hated that show. I hated him. It took every ounce of anger in me to force myself to stand there in that closet and bear that stink, to wait like a stalking cat. The hatchet got wet and slippery in my hand, but I held it tighter and tighter.

Then the door opened. I got ready. This was it. I knew it was gonna happen. There was no other way.

Mario shut the door behind him. He came two steps into the trailer before it got him. He raised his hand to his nose.

"What the fuck is that smell?" he whispered to himself. He retched and went to steady his heaving stomach. He was going to vomit.

I was a foot away. I opened the closet door and split the back of Mario's head in half with the hatchet. He dropped like a sack of shit. I quickly picked up his gun. The television was blaring away. Letterman was saying something idiotic, playing the fool. I could hear his cackling, moronic laugh.

I stepped into the bedroom. William looked up at me. He was naked, and on his fat, hairy belly rested a white, clean hand with slender fingers and long red fingernails.

Velena.

"We're trying to watch television!" Stinky William whined to me in an angry, condescending voice.

Velena stood and wrapped a towel around her naked body.

"Do it," she said.

I plugged him in the head. He didn't even move. He just lazily had his head blown open in bed. Perfect.

Velena came to my side.

I was not expecting her to be there. "Go to the sink, get the money, and bring it to me," I told her. She did as she was told.

"What are we gonna do with the bodies?" she asked.

"Nevermind." I gave her the keys to my van. "Meet me at Pike River in about four hours."

***

Four hours later I was riding my Dickie Dee cart up to Pike River at four in the morning on a warm, August night. I had close to twenty thousand fat ones in a knapsack on my back and about 400-plus pounds of hacked-up human flesh in the belly of my ice cream cart. It was hard peddling, I'll tell you that, but it was gonna be worth it when I dumped the cart in the deepest part of the river.

My plan was this: I would take the cart around to the back of the swamp where there was an old bridge and toss the cart off into the deep mucky lake, locking the latch so the bodies would never float to the surface. Then I would coach Velena to get our stories straight: "Mario showed up and left with William. We haven't seen either one of them since."

I would clean the blood out of the trailer, get Velena in the shower, and finally hide the twenty grand in the marsh in a water-proof bucket. I would pick it up in the fall and everything would be jake. Lem would take it out on Nicky the Italian in the Airstream and assume that he'd taken the money.

As I peddled up the final hill to the bridge over Pike River, my heart jingling and ringing like the bells on the Dickie Dee cart, I saw my van.

Good girl, Velena, I thought. We were gonna get away with it.

I pushed the ice cream cart over into the bushes and ran up to the van. "We did it, baby," I said, opening the passenger door to jump in, but I stopped because there was someone already in the seat.

"How's it going, Candy Man?" Lem Lowry said. He wasn't wearing his sheriff's uniform, just jeans and a black T-shirt. "I want you to listen to what I'm gonna tell you," Lem said. He motioned over to Velena. "You've met my maid, haven't you?"

"You fucker," I spat.

"Blood's on your hands now, Candy. Gimme the knapsack," Lem ordered as he pulled out a Saturday Night Special and pointed it at my chest. He looked up at the sky, the stars. "Nice night, eh?"

"How could you do that to her?" I handed the knapsack over to Lem. "How could you do that to yourself?" I yelled at Velena.

"I figured somebody would kill William eventually," Lem told me. "Either you or the ginos. Just took a little prodding from Velena. Course I didn't expect you to kill William *and* Mario. Fuck, did you fly off the handle or what? Smart guy would have just let Mario kill William and then killed Mario. Pleaded self-defense."

He was right, of course, and it pissed me off even worse. "You think you are so fucking smart! You pimp sonofabitch! How could you do that to her?"

"Shut up, dummy," Lem snapped me off. He opened the knapsack and whistled at the near twenty large in hundred dollar bills inside.

"Well, Candy, think of it this way: at least you got your trailer back. But I wouldn't be getting too comfortable. Mario was part of the Galiano family. I saw him on "America's Most Wanted." When Nicky Galiano finds out that Mario has been murdered, Nicky'll be all over you like stink on William. You killed his only brother."

"What am I gonna do?"

"Get in. We'll drive you out of town. Then you're on your own." Lem led me around to the back of the van, his gun jammed into my ribs. He pulled out some twine and tied my wrists before he opened the van and helped me inside. He then tied my feet and shut the doors. From the driver's seat, Velena turned around and smiled at me.

"You did good. You did real good," she said. "Almost got away with it, but Lem's too smart."

"How could you let him do this to you? How could you do that to yourself? It's disgusting. How could you sleep in that fat pig's bed?"

"You don't know what it's like to love, Candy Man. Your heart is full of hate, and that's all you know. People will do anything for love." She smiled at Lem as he opened the passenger seat door and climbed into the van. "He's going to buy me a diamond ring and we'll be married. He loves me."

Lem smiled back at me with his crooked, evil smile and grey eyes. I knew it would be a miracle if Velena lived till dawn.

"Put that tape on, baby," Lem told her.

Velena pushed a cassette tape into the stereo. "The Candy Man can 'cause he mixes it with love and makes the world taste good ..."

Velena drove off into the night. They were both singing. My Dickie Dee cart was still sitting in the brush. I could have sworn I saw blood dripping onto the tire.

Lem reached over and kissed Velena on the cheek. "Ohh," Lem scowled waving his hand in front of his nose. "You need a shower, baby."

Rita Carter

BY JESS DUKES

Rita Carter somehow found out about her clitoris when the rest of us were still arguing over stickers that smelled like real buttered popcorn. Maybe she didn't know the technical word for it, but she knew a few moves.

When I was twelve, I spent the night with Rita for the first time, where I learned all sorts of things. After Rita's parents told us to go to bed, we giggled for twenty minutes before I realized that Rita had her huge stuffed pig in a clutch. She was lying on her back, arms and legs wrapped around that pig, arms and legs rocking north and south. She was still giggling. I stared at the dark blue shadows on her walls. Then she gave me my own stuffed animal, and I rolled around with it for a few minutes while Rita and I talked about which teachers we didn't like. I didn't know what I was doing, or why. Rita laughed at me.

By the time we started high school, Rita discovered brushes. Her parents thought she had a bad case of teen vanity, but really, Rita was collecting the handles. They had big ridges, tiny ridges, and no ridges. They were curved and straight. She even had a brush with a handle shaped like Santa and couldn't wait to whisper her desires to the same man at the mall come Christmas.

One night, I was sleeping over, and I was sitting with the Carters in the TV room, waiting on Rita. I guess she didn't prepare the handle well enough, because that night she picked a big one. And it stuck. Every five minutes, Rita's mom yelled at her to get her ass moving. Rita yelled back, "I'm moving my ass!" but never came downstairs. Finally, Rita yelled out my name.

I got to Rita's door and she was whimpering. "It's too fucking big," she said, starting to cry. By now, Rita had a good grip on cussing, too. She could bring any boy in school to his knees with one good vocabulary word. She was always so ahead of her time. *Very* adult. Maybe that's why I didn't know what to do to help her. She moved her skirt up her leg, and I could see the black plastic prongs of the brush standing ramrod straight up against her thighs. "My stomach hurts," she said.

"Just pull it out," I said, sitting beside her on the bed.

"Fuck. Don't you think I tried that?" She pulled her skirt all the way up to her waist and pushed on the brush lodged between her legs like a pole in cement.

"Stand up. Relax. Maybe it will just fall out," I said.

"It hurts to stand up. It hurts my stomach." Rita really started to cry. I noticed there was blood on the bed, and then I started to cry. I went back downstairs and whispered to Rita's mom that something was wrong and to not be mad at Rita. And that Rita was crying. Rita's mom ran upstairs, and a minute later we all heard a shriek. It sounded like, "*What the fuck*??"

A second after that, we all heard Rita screaming, "Stop pulling!"

Rita and her mom came down the stairs, Rita wrapped in a sheet and sweating. They didn't even stop to explain. They limped right through the TV room into the garage and took off. The Carter boys looked dumb; it had all happened so fast. "I'm going home," I said.

Turns out the brush handle, which was hollow with a hole at one end, created a perfect vacuum. By the time a doctor cut it out, her whole family knew what Rita was up to—and they assumed she was up to it with me. The Carters still look at me sideways. The vision of their daughter's sawed-up hairbrush will always remind them of me. Rita said she didn't want to see me anymore.

***

The next year, I got my first boyfriend. Jack was a year older than me, but I impressed him with a story about a girl I knew who once loved a stuffed pig. Jack and I started kissing every morning before class. Then we added kissing at lunch. Then we added kissing while waiting for the buses after school. Then we started sneaking out of class so we could run off to the woods next to the school on the one side of the building where, institutionally, there were absolutely no windows.

One day in the woods, Jack asked me if I wanted to watch him. I thought he was going to do something stupid like climb a tree and hang upside down, so I said, "sure." But instead, he started unzipping his pants. He barely got his underwear to his knees when the bell rang. I watched him pack his ass back into his jeans and we made plans to meet at his house that afternoon.

Jack knew a lot about his sperm. He ate oysters and turkey every week for the zinc. He said it made his sperm stronger. I didn't know if he meant that they would be stronger for when he'd need to get someone pregnant, or if they would be stronger tasting, or if they would be stronger smelling ... but I didn't ask. I nodded like

I knew what he was talking about and then I distracted him with more kissing.

Soon, kissing was not enough for Jack. Every afternoon, we'd soak the sofa in the basement of his building with spit and sperm and whatever was coming out of me. Rita had taught me a thing or two, but something still wasn't exactly right. I didn't squirm the way she did, but Jack seemed to like what I did, anyway. He, on the other hand, knew what he was doing with himself.

Jack stole porno magazines from the video store on the other side of town. He told me about an article he read where people made fake vaginas out of sandwich bags filled with jelly. They put the bag between two pillows, wrap their legs around the whole kit, and rock back and forth. "It's too messy, though," Jack said. I distracted him with more kissing.

Jack's sperm, as it turned out, were really strong. They were so strong, they could fly. They flew right through the air. Jack liked an audience too, so I made sure he knew how thrilling his act was. "That's fucking fantastic," I'd tell him. By now, I was pretty good at cussing too. Between kissing and rolling around and touching each other and cussing, we stayed busy over the next few months.

Jack became an expert. After about an hour of showing off for me, he'd explode. He'd lie flat on his back on the dirty couch with his head hanging off of one side so that all the blood could rush to his face and make him dizzy. I usually sat on one of his legs so that he didn't fall off. At the end, his super strong sperm crashed onto his chest. It hit him on the shoulder. If he looked up, he could catch his own mess right in the face. Usually, he kept his head bent back and the sperm would land on the concrete floor behind him. I always made sure I saw where it landed so that we wouldn't slip in it later.

One afternoon, Jack lay on the sofa, watching me take off my jeans. His right arm was working up and down.

"Are we ever going to have sex?" he asked.

"Jack. You know I'm a virgin," I reminded him.

"Okay. Fine. But will you at least stick something inside?"

I thought about Rita. "Why don't we wait until next year? You'll probably have your own car by then. Let's save it for the car."

That day, Jack's sperm hit him in the eye. The next day, he broke up with me. His eye was pink and irritated.

***

Without Jack, I had a lot of time on my hands. Most nights, I hung my head off the side of my bed and felt around, wondering if I really was like a sandwich bag full of jelly on the inside. I thought a lot about Rita, too. I wished her parents would stop hating me.

Soon enough, I told myself I was going to have a real orgasm, just like Rita and Jack. I began to push myself up against anything that I could find: the edge of my mattress, the doorjamb, the cold tile wall in the bathroom, the remote control buttons—anything was fair game. All I had to do was close my eyes and think of Rita's stuffed pig and Jack's basement. I wanted what they had.

Nikki, a friend of mine from school, told me about the shower massager at her house. I didn't have one, so for a week, I staggered around in front of my parents, acting like I had a terrible neck pain. They bought me a heating pad and some Icy Hot gel, which felt great between my legs and made my lap smell like a dinner mint, but still didn't do the trick. After the second week, my mom started massaging my neck. This was obviously a step in the wrong direction, so I quit the act.

At school, I told Nikki how I failed to get my parents to buy me a shower massager. "It's a shame," Nicola said. "It would definitely do the trick." Then she told me another way. I ran straight home to try it.

Hanging my head off the side of the bed is nothing compared to the weightlessness of lying at the bottom of a full bathtub. The water from the faucet was warm like spit. I planted my heels on the wall. Underwater, I held on to the side of the tub; I was slipping around too much and the water wasn't getting its chance with me. I finally got a hold of the right combination of wet and dry surfaces to hold myself in one place. I closed my eyes.

The water ran at me like a charging bull and lights fired around my eyes in the dark. I thought I was about to slip away because my legs were shaking, but I held on. My hair floated all around me. Then I froze. And I was deaf. My eyes were open, but I was blind. And I was shooting fire out of my hips. My ankles disappeared and my knees were as heavy as boulders.

I was almost in a headstand, but didn't know it. I was so excited, my face slipped underwater and took a deep, deep breath.

I always thought that dying during sex would be the worst way to go, slightly worse than dying on the toilet. I managed to drag myself to the edge of the bathtub before I passed out. The water overflowed and ran out into the hallway, which brought my brother into the bathroom. He yelled for my mother and I only remember coughing and spitting up foamy water. The fire between my legs was gone. My family stood in a few inches of water. We eventually moved out of that apartment. And they never did get a shower massager.

Everyone's a Critic

BY JAY BRIDA

Even though I was dazed by the effects of breaking through the wall, as it was called, I was still aware enough to know how good the gun felt pressed up to my body.

It was erotic and horribly empowering. My body prickled, and I knew I was wet even though I had been a pacifist my entire life. I was the president of my campus NOW chapter. I volunteered for Stop Handguns Now in the early 90's. Now, though, I found myself fingering the cool metal like I was teasing it before it came in my face.

Even better than the cool, priapic gat rubbing up against my left nipple however, was the primal feeling of being on the hunt. I had hit the programmed mark and found myself, as expected, on Ludlow Street in the Lower East Side, waiting for the scene to play out.

I turned the corner onto Houston and looked in a large window. There they were, right on cue. A perky blonde with a button nose and weird, geri-curled white-girl hair, sitting with some putrid nebbish with a receding hairline and sandpaper growth for a beard. The woman had always annoyed me, the poster girl for all women who felt they needed a man to validate their lives. She was the proto-McBeal. All status and needs. And I hated her fucking guts.

The guy, on the other hand, was a conscious shtick played in corduroy. He was nothing but a series of painful, annoying tics with terrible hair who pretended to be a humane-yet-still-honest, cool-eyed broker of the human condition.

I wanted both of them dead.

Something more than déjà vu hit me. I had seen this scene a half-dozen times. I had imagined myself in this very position a half-dozen more. Still, it was a bit unnerving. I wasn't prepared for the smell, particularly. Somehow, the noxious scent of burnt metal was still in my nostrils from my trip through the slipstream. Mix that with the heavy, aged smell of hot dogs and pastrami, and I felt that I might spew, ruining my chance at redemption.

Instead of attacking directly, I took some time to collect myself by concentrating on how well I actually knew this place: the ocher grease accumulations over the grill, the unconvincing vinyl plywood paneling on every wall, the uniformed counter staff. I reached a state of near transcendence, having visualized and mapped out my present and future. I mean, it *had* to play out the way it was going to ... until I entered the scene.

That was when I had creative control. Since I knew how this was going to play out, I had a total advantage. It would be better played to pick my moment—and my style. A gun was too conventional. It wasn't really dramatic enough, or maybe it was too clichéd. When I thought about it, I felt it didn't rise to the moment.

So, I improvised while I waited for the inevitable shrieking climax to their idiotic conversation.

While the cooks and waitstaff became distracted by the woman's absurd histrionics, I steeled myself and made a move, creeping behind the counter, swiping a serrated knife from the counter. I maneuvered around the gawking customers, whose attentions were fixed squarely on the woman's bucking and moans.

At the height of her fake orgasm, as her head fell back in faux spasms, I grabbed her hair and drew the blade across her neck, digging in as hard as I could, making a clean, straight, deep cut across her throat.

"How's that, bitch?" I said with a manic quiver in my voice. I pumped her head back and forth. "You sniveling narcissist. Men are your problem? You are *our* problem, you insufferable cunt."

I let out a guttural, fearsome howl.

"You want what *she's* having, you crusty old gash?" I menaced my knife at a woman a table away.

Sally was gurgling and spilling blood into her perfectly arranged salad. Harry sat stunned, his fish mouth agape. Thinking about that ugly, pursed motherfucking mouth filled me with an incandescent hate that was a million times more feral than the angriest grudge fuck I'd ever mustered.

In one smooth movement, I pounced on the table—kicking a plate of pickles across Katz's Deli—jumped on top of Harry —knocking him flat on his back—and pulled out my perfectly polished, glimmering silver Smith and Wesson. I paused for a moment to appreciate how quickly the smugness vanished from his puckered face, and then I focused on that hideous mouth. I stuck my gun in, closed my eyes, and heard a wet, thick explosion.

I think I tasted brain.

"Anyone else?!"

I turned and faced the rest of the restaurant, aiming my gun into the crowd. They complied by cringing and screaming.

My mission done, I made a quick line to the door, turned back down Ludlow St. and, once out of sight, I turned a copper bracelet on my wrist. And I was gone.

Now, there *are* rules. My roommate, who turned me on to breaking the wall, gave me the list:

1. Real people don't die. But you might.

You're not killing *people*, per se, you are killing characters. Fictional characters in shitty movies. Fictional characters in popular movies who drive you fucking crazy. Fictional characters in popular movies who drive you fucking crazy while they help make things worse for humanity. There was no crew, no off-camera. You are hermetically sealed in the movie, impacting the *movie's* reality, but not ours. That said, if you do get killed in the movie, you will be dead, so choose your roles carefully.

2. It may or may not change the movie as we know it.

This rule, it seems, contradicts Rule #1, but it doesn't really. Relativity being what it is, your actions affect the movie, and could affect existing copies or airings of the movie that were already made—the movie in a parallel universe. This may be a difficult concept to grasp, but stay with the premise. This is why the resolution to the central plot of *Twin Peaks*—Who killed Laura Palmer?—made no sense whatsoever. However, this was our first attempt, and it was an artistic and political failure. As a result, we hardly do television anymore.

3. Don't humanize the characters.

While they look and sound like the actors playing them, they are not the actors. They are perfect doppelgangers, with the motivations, pasts, and presents of the characters they play. Do not think of them by their actor names, only their character names.

4. You are a revolutionary agent, act like it.

Aim high. There are too many bad movies with inessential characters. Killing them does not make a statement, nor does it make the cumulative impact of breaking the wall a worthwhile endeavor. Our goal is to change the subtext of these movies through the revolutionary act of changing the universal and thematic essence. It is our belief that a collective effort, over time, will ultimately change the entire dynamic of cinema and storytelling. This leads us to #5.

5. Jar-Jar Binks.

Somehow George Lucas thought it would be a good idea to introduce a pidgin-talking, shuffling minstrel into his *Star Wars* movies. However, as he is entirely a digital creation, right down to his exaggerated Sambo lips, he is out of our reach. We could be convinced he would be a worthy target, if he had an actual physical manifestation.

6. We don't know what we don't know.

Breaking the wall is an applied hypothesis still being tested. Unanticipated events can and will occur. We just don't know what they are yet. That said, if any breaker runs afoul of the above rules or deviates from the spirit of our mission, steps will be taken to address the problem.

***

After killing Sally, I had sworn off another direct action, as the few breakers I knew called it, at least for awhile. It was true, as my roommate had warned me, that the immediate, visceral nature of it was appalling, but what she didn't mention (and something that was far more disturbing to me)—it was also immensely arousing. Once I had exited the picture and come back home, I felt a deep and unquenchable need for raw fucking.

I was in the throes of a shivering, epic, seemingly unquenchable lust when I found my roommate sleeping sideways on the couch, exactly where I had left her minutes before. I had only been gone for about four minutes of screen time. It had seemed much longer.

I stood over her for a moment, tracing out the arch of her lower back with my eyes, moving up her exposed midriff to her breasts. She stirred a little on the couch, which momentarily paralyzed me and shocked me into the reality of the moment. It did not, however, diminish my hunger.

I did a quick calculus. She wasn't gay. I wasn't gay. She was my roommate. I was in heat. The answer came fast.

I straddled her hip as my left leg slid quickly between her ass and the couch, and my right leg snaked around her. She woke up as I started to grind my soaked pussy into her.

"What the fuck?" she said, trying to wriggle free. But I wasn't having it.

"Don't move," I said quietly, maintaining my pace. "Don't ... fucking ... move."

My clit kept running over a rivet on her jeans. The pain that came with it aroused me even more. I lowered my body a little, to catch more of her pelvis. I was grinding so hard into the rivet on top of her right front pocket, concentrating, that I wasn't quite sure if she was moving with *me* or *against* me. And I didn't much care; it was the movement that counted.

When the friction started to heat my pussy, I went over the edge. I threw her around and straddled her belt, while pinning her hands above her hair. She looked at me. Her face was calm, but her body shifted, I thought, ever so slightly under mine. I scraped across the large clasp of her belt with as much pressure as I could muster.

"I want to fuck."

"So fuck," she said.

I shifted my hands around so I could grab both of her wrists in one hand. With my free hand, I unbuckled my belt, unzipped my pants and slid my hand through my slick, saturated pubic hair while continuing to buck on my roommate's belt. It wasn't enough. I needed more. I got off my roommate and took off my pants and panties, leaving myself naked from the waist down.

There was a pause. I felt a creeping measure of regret.

"You know, when I got back, I had a craving for cake," my roommate said.

"So what did you do?" I asked, still slightly panting, and noticing a warm trickle running down my leg.

"I made a cake."

She got up and stood with her face to me. I wasn't sure if she was going to kiss me or hit me. I craved either option.

"I'm not a cake," she said finally and walked out of the room.

I went into my room, lay down on my bed and stared at the ceiling. My ride had stopped.

About an hour later, I heard a faint knock on the door.

"Yeah?"

"Got a minute?" my roommate asked.

"I'm sorry. Really. I'd just rather not talk about it."

"Yeah, me neither. Got a minute?"

"Come in," I said.

She entered. It was obvious she had let it go.

"What about *Forrest Gump*?"

I looked at her and grinned.

Forrest Gump. Goddamn right, *Forrest Gump.* My craving for a taste of that sugar-sweet blood made me feel like a diabetic vampire.

Gump. The slow-witted, unspeakably stupid, All-American poster boy. Perfect. In that world, philosophy was replaced by inane platitudes. Intellectualism was a death sentence. The female-lead Jenny? A one-time college radical who fell into drugs, felt suicidal listening to Lynyrd Skynyrd, slept around, and then got AIDS —only after pity-fucking the mentally handicapped. Pamela DesBarres is alive, but this idiot would die of AIDS?

From a revolutionary standpoint, he was a perfect target. Stupidity is pure. Thinking for yourself will make you terminally miserable, then kill or cripple you.

I made my tracking calculations, knew to avoid the storm and war scenes and settled on a plan. I jerry-rigged a trip wire on a deserted strip of highway that ignited two "jumping" land mines on each side of the road. I got Gump on his return jog across the country and I got to watch, joining the pack somewhere near Monument Valley. In a nice, if unexpected, twist, the followers he had accumulated on his run committed mass suicide.

***

The need for sexual gratification came flooding back after my *Gump* mission. My roommate had made it clear, however, that her hip, lips, and points south were off-limits. Instead, I invested in a sliver metal vibrator. I think I gave my clit nerve damage through a buzzing overuse, but it was close to what I needed.

I had thought about scouting for a boyfriend or a regular screw, but I became increasingly interested in administering cinematic justice and less interested in everything else. Mission.

Completion. Orgasm. My life outside the wall, back in "reality," was in shambles.

After the *Desperately Seeking Susan* operation, my roommate moved out in protest and I became so preoccupied by various actions, I was fired from my job at the commercial post-production studio.

Worse, the longer it lasted, the less aroused and less interested in the political end of things I became. I started to have purely aesthetic arguments with the few other breakers I came into contact with.

I despised what I thought were purposely joyless, prim efforts from European directors. I thought Japanese horror was utterly overrated (not that you'd catch me in *that* minefield), and I couldn't stand Rob Zombie. This branded me a counter-revolutionary among some of the enthusiasts of what I considered the cinema of pain.

In reaction to their formalism, I began to "festival" my work. I killed Detective Mike Dooley in *K-9* and its two sequels by giving the dog cop a shot of rabies and unleashing him on his partner. I smothered Rhett Butler in his sleep, then Inman as he left *Cold Mountain* (where I contracted malaria), saving him the horror of watching his friends die. I finished up my Redneck Trilogy by slicing open Larry with a cleaver during his riff on a Chinese restaurant in *Larry the Cable Guy: Health Inspector*. I wiped out everyone in the Nora Ephron oeuvre, going back twice for the entire *Sleepless in Seattle* cast, first cutting off their eyelids. The second time, I think I just poisoned them. Then there was my "Stranglish the *Spanglish*" mission, which I thought had merit.

But it wasn't always inspired work. Often, I'd find myself doing an Oswald—sniping characters from rooftops or open windows—safely out of view, but it counted the same. Or so I told myself.

Inter-dimensional travel started to warp and blur the boundaries between my reality and the scenes I was participating in. I started noticing contemporary graffiti for Good Charlotte and Nas in the hallways while on my commando raid on *The Breakfast Club* (I decided to pick them off one by one, like an Agatha Christie novella. I got Claire by lacing her lipstick with concentrated arsenic. I picked off Brian when he went to tell the principal that Claire was convulsing, Andy with a hatchet to the top of his spinal column when he went to check on Brian, Allison with a gun at close range, then Bender with the gun in his hand, which then "proved" that he was guilty of a quadruple homicide/suicide. With a home life like his, few were surprised). Likewise, there was a dramatic increase in continuity goofs: people's gloves would instantly change hands, soda cans would be there one second, disappear the next, clocks ran in spasms with no correlation to the running time. Worse still, with the feeling of catharsis gone, breaking the wall became just another bag job.

I had long since disposed of the rules. I aimed high and low. I killed for no reason, and I killed just to screw with the fabric of the movie—by killing inessential characters, scenes ground to a halt. Plus, I humanized the characters left and right—I made love to Erin Brockovich, calling her Julia the whole time, before sparing her life altogether. I had affairs with Rufus T. Firefly, Frank Serpico, and Tom Hagen just to see how they fucked.

But it was only after shoving an ice pick into Catherine Trammell's left eye (after *my* orgasm, thank you very much) to get a measure of ironic revenge for her psycho-lesbo shtick in *Basic Instinct* that I started noticing the same people in mission after mission. They weren't atmospheric extras. They weren't characters at all. They didn't interact with the scene; they would just be around, looking at me, sometimes taking notes.

What was supposed to be a radical correction of the artistic markets had spun wildly out of control. I was led to understand that my solo revolution was coming to an end.

When I got back home from *Basic Instinct's* San Francisco, I weighed my options. The first was to quit, and it was even the right option to take, but I knew the truth: I was too far gone. There was no life to go back to.

I looked around my apartment. There were DVDs everywhere. My TiVO machine was recording something I had forgotten I programmed. I had even spent my last remaining $1,000 on a BlueRay player, just for the ratio quality. For food, I had exactly one small jar of mustard and a box of baking powder.

No, it was the revolution or bust. And since I had suspected that other breakers were unifying against me, I chose the Tony Montana route. There was, after all, romance in making a last stand.

I hacked into a Hollywood gossip blog, and reported the scenarios I had lived out. Most readers took them to be revenge fantasies. But in the meantime, I found out what characters they found worthy of death, and what movies had driven them to the point of homicide.

These were tricky shoals, of course. The most passionate types were fanboys pissed at Peter Jackson for leaving their favorite wizard out of some massive war scene or some such thing. And I didn't want to get in the middle of the Kirk vs. Picard wars. Then there was Jar-Jar. At least everyone wanted Jar-Jar gutted and bleeding.

But there were some original ideas. Picking off a cast of meddling kids while they were trying to solve a witless "mystery" was smart. Jennifer Love Hewitt was a popular target, especially for women ... but again, it was her they wanted dead, not any particular character. I had to explain that I'd put a chainsaw to Adam Sandler if I could, but that wasn't in the spirit of the revolution.

There was one suggestion, though, that caught my attention. It was a film I hadn't yet entered, one with a suitable subversion factor, one that I fucking loathed. I made up my mind and started the usual prep work.

***

For this mission, I was armed to the teeth. I made several test runs to learn the contours of the settings and the tools I would have at my disposal, to stash the weapons I took in and figure out which marks they would hit—it was definitely a *they* kind of job. I even read a fan site that went into excruciating detail about procedural trivia.

It felt like the good old days. With a slick heat spreading up from my crotch, I was revitalized by the righteousness of the mission. I decided to insinuate myself into the plot of the thing, too, for a change.

With a simple load and lock, I was gone. My first stop was Dr. Charlie Blackwood's office at Miramar. She had to be first for my plan to work. The mission here was to kill her, dispose of her body where it would not be found, *and* make myself into a credible military tactician.

Unfortunately, I missed my mark by seconds, putting me in a strange hallway somewhere on the base. I had to make a quick calculation. While I was dressed for the part—hair in a bun, the blousiest blouse I could find, heavy black-rimmed rectangular glasses, prim grey skirt, heels—and had a perfectly forged ID pinned to my chest, I felt very conspicuous walking around a Navy facility. I first had to get my bearings, then formulate a new plan of attack.

I walked down an antiseptic hallway, turned a corner, then walked down another that was identical to the first. Out of the corner of my eye, I saw a familiar face in an office writing something into a notebook.

Paranoia started to creep in. My walking became faster. The echoes of my clip-clopping heels made me even more aware of my fraudulent presence here. I turned one more corner and there she was. I met her chest-on-chest, both of us surprised; she, because we were dressed alike right down to a replica of her identification tag, me, because I couldn't reach the butcher knife I had stowed away in her office.

"Hello," she said.

I figured she hadn't yet seen my name tag.

"Hi." I sounded hesitant, weak. "Say, you don't look like the typical instructor at Miramar!"

"Neither do you."

I looked down the hallway. It was empty.

"Yeah, I hear that all the time. What's your name?"

"Dr. Charlotte Blackwood."

I laughed out loud.

"What's funny about that?"

I wanted to say, "The plot, you twat! What the fuck would you know about fighter jets? Why do you think you're here, anyway?" but I stammered something idiotic about how I had a friend named Blackwood who was funny.

She eventually got around me to walk down the hallway I had just left. Shaking, I walked a few steps before I noticed her office door. I hadn't recognized the hallway because I had only been *inside* her office to drop off my weapon.

"Dr. Blackwood!" I yelled.

"Yes?"

"I'm sorry. Could you meet me in your office here for a moment?"

"Yes?" she said. There was uncertainty in her voice.

I went in and looked behind the filing cabinet where I had taped my hunting knife. It was still there. She barged in, her eyes flaring.

"Can I help you?" She was angry. I was falling in love with her. I began to lose my nerve about the whole thing.

"Maverick seems gay, doesn't he?" I said.

"What?"

"Maverick. He's with Goose. They're gay, right?"

"Who are you talking about?"

I had made a rookie mistake, a continuity goof in real time. I had forgotten the plot entirely. She was obviously on her way to address her class for the first time, and Maverick didn't approach her until *after* the class scene.

"And why are you wearing my name tag?"

I casually did a pirouette and put on my best coy face.

"I'm calling security."

I reached behind the cabinet and ripped off my knife. She looked up from dialing to find me jumping over the desk between us. She tried to put her arms up, but I managed to gash her just under her ear. She staggered back with a free flow of blood splattering against the floor. This was bad. Blood tends to get noticed. Charlie was still mute, leaning against the wall, looking at me with exaggerated, terror-filled eyes.

"Oh, don't give me that look," I said. I held the knife up to her throat. "Stay quiet, pretty."

I unbuttoned her shirt with one hand while maintaining my metal pressure on her throat. "Shhhh ..."

I rolled the shirt in my hands and gagged her with it. I then ripped out the phone chord and wrapped her arms behind her. I forced her to sit in the chair—she appeared to be losing consciousness by this point—and I looped the chord around her, knotting it to a bolt I found in the floor.

"Stay fucking quiet, bitch," I said, leaving for class.

It wasn't until I was facing a class of "hotshot" Top Gun pilots that I was alerted to the blood around my crotch. The bitch had bled on me.

"Hey, uh, Doc," Iceman said. "You forgetting something today, like your tampon?"

That was their opening line. The assembled studs found it hilariously funny.

I had fucked up this mission from the start. I knew I had only one chance—a full-on freak out to ice all of the boys at once. I wouldn't be able to do-in Goose's adorable wife. I wouldn't be able to peg their flight positions for the Russian MiGs. I wasn't going to be able to point out their unbelievable homoeroticism on the volleyball court, nor was I going to be able to take their machismo head-on by castrating Maverick when he started singing to me at that bar. A balls-out blitzkrieg was the only way to salvage anything out of the operation.

I feigned embarrassment at the blood and went to sit down at the desk, under which I kept an Uzi.

They continued on the menstrual blood kick.

"You know, Goose, when I end a sentence, I don't end it with an exclamation point," Maverick said in a stage voice.

"Oh, no?" Goose answered.

"No, for me, it's all about the period."

A porcelain forest of teeth shone in my face. He wasn't laughing, just smiling. Smug. With immense self-satisfaction.

I bent down to get the gun. Just as I reached for it, I was tackled from the side. My chair flipped over and I became disoriented.

"No!" a voice shouted.

While I was sprawled on the floor, I noticed a look of surprise on Maverick's face. Some of the men got up out of their chairs, some stayed. One said, "Oh, cool, cat fight!"

I was on my stomach as my attacker sat on my shoulders, punching me in the back of the head. The Uzi was only a few feet from my reach.

As I began to lose consciousness, my thoughts clarified. There was the pain, of course. But then there was a sense of calm, too. The pain allowed me to piece together the randomness into something deeper, something whole. I realized this was what I was probably supposed to do all along. I should have made my own damn movie.

A few hours later, I came to, feeling the shrieking throb of the headache that had been beaten into me. I was in a small cell. My ex-roommate sat in a chair on the other side of the bars.

I sat up, rubbing my head.

"This your work?" I asked as my hand matted my hair into a thick knot.

"Yeah," she said. "You're in the brig on the base."

"So, now what?"

"I don't know. You pissed a lot of people off, here and on the other side."

"Did I at least unravel the plot?"

"I guess."

I noticed that my bracelet was gone, meaning I was stuck in this brig until ... well, until forever, I supposed.

"Why did you come for me?"

"I like this movie."

She stood and turned the copper bracelet on her wrist. It was odd how she disappeared. There was a flicker, her figure faded in and out, and then she was gone.

Attack of the Deer

BY CARL MOORE

I knelt down in front of the ink, squirting it into deer shapes on her tights.

"They'll run all over if you let 'em," she said.

I looked over my shoulder, imagining the black outlines of the animals bounding through the brick rooms, escaping from where we'd drawn them.

"If they did that, they'd be art thieves. They'd be stealing themselves," I said.

"No, I meant the drops of ink. Did you think I meant the deer? They hardly even look like deer," she said.

"I guess they don't," I said, frowning over the thin antlers, the hints at bodies.

"It's okay, you're only doing this to relax. I'm going to give you these tights."

I nodded, picked the tights up off the worktable, and left, figuring I'd overstayed my welcome in Montana's apartment. Slipping out the front door of her downstairs boutique, I walked out onto Broadway, followed it under the train track, winding my way through the crowds and cars. It must have been eighty or ninety degrees, but it felt like 800.

I noticed a deer was following me—a shaggy sweat-ball of a thing that I suspected was some underpaid jerk in a deer costume. He caught up with me at the light, straightened up, and blinked his black, conjunctivitic eyes.

"Hey boss, you spare a dollar?" he asked.

"I'm not your boss," I said. "I haven't been at my job or seen my fiancée in four days. In fact, I may not have either one anymore, and I'm running out of couches to surf on."

"Fifty cents?"

I sighed, handed him the tights. "Here, I was going to give these to her. You can sell 'em."

The light turned green and I crossed the street, headed past the McDonald's, Dunkin' Donuts, Taco Bell, and Penny Lenny's Dollar Discount. I finally stopped to check out the menu in the window of a Latin diner where a group of young Puerto Rican guys sat around drinking beers and eating beans. Beyond them, a short deer stood at the bar drinking a margarita and gluing his eyes to the waitress' ass.

"I like the way you move, Mami," said the deer.

She shouted in rapid Spanish, stamped her foot, and ended it with, "Get the hell out!"

The deer hopped off the stool and, strutting on his hind legs, walked out under the watchful glare of the men at the table.

"She's uptight, huh?" he asked me.

"I don't know her. Or you," I said.

"You gotta dollar, boss?" the first deer asked the second.

The second deer gave him five dollars then tapped me on the shoulder with his hoof as a tall, red-haired woman in a backless dress drifted by us.

"Wow, you see her swingin' that ass? I'd break off a few antlers for her." He shook his head in emphasis. It was quite a rack, twelve points at a quick count, and way too large for his stubby, muscular body. Around his neck he wore a silver chain with a large, diamond-studded *D*.

"Les' go talk to 'er," he said, looping his hoof through my arm and following the woman into a laundromat. "Hey Red," he called out, "look at me."

The woman turned, eyebrows furrowing at the sight of us.

"I got a big rack for a little buck, and I was hopin' you did, too. Know what I mean?"

"Are you guys peace protesters or something?" she asked.

"Nah, we're just outta luck. You got a dollar?" asked the first deer.

"If I give it to you, will you go away?" she asked.

"Oh yeah, you can give to me," said the second deer, "on the floor, on the table, in the freakin' washing machine, baby."

"Look, I'm sorry," I said to the woman. "They dragged me in here."

"No, it's okay, but this is some kind of art thing, right? Some performance thing?" She was looking up and around, like someone had planted cameras on the ceiling.

"I wish it was," I said.

"Hey, look," said the second deer. "Door's open in the back, let's check it out." He beckoned with his hoof, pointed with his snout.

The woman took a few cautious steps toward the door, trying to peer around the corner, figuring this was the spot where the camera crew was hiding.

"Come on, it's all right, I ain't gonna harm ya or nuthin', it's cool baby, you got a name, baby?"

"Brenda," she said.

"Oh, you got a pretty name, Brenda. I'm D-Deer. You mighta seen me at the diner down the street?"

"No."

"Well they all know me in there, the waitresses and stuff. But come on, let's see what's back here ... hey, look, some trees. I love trees. I'm a deer, know what I mean?"

She giggled as he shook his white tail and bounded over the dryers. He stuck his snout on the glass door, made a print, then licked it off. She laughed more, called him cute, then he disappeared around the corner. His tail reappeared for a little shake, then vanished again with the girl following eagerly.

"I don't know if I want to go back there," I said.

"Yeah, me neither," said the first deer. "Hey, I bet that guy standing over by the cash register has some money."

"The cashier?"

"Yeah, the cashier. Let's go near the cashier."

"And do what?"

"I don't know," he said, then walked over to the cash register and stood there, hitting up the customers for a dollar when they got their change, walking a few paces away when the cashier glared at him.

I didn't know what to do. I didn't want to associate with the deer anymore. I had to get outside again, outside and away. If only the whole neighborhood didn't hang out in the doorway, I could push through.

"Yeah, push through, man. Just push through," came the whisper in my ear. I felt a wet muzzle on the back of my neck and a damp spindly body clinging to my shoulders.

"Who's there?" I asked, spinning around.

"Just Getouttahair."

"I'm trying to."

"No," came the frail whisper. "It's Getouttahair Deer. I can't stop trying to get outta wherever I am. I mean, as soon as we get outta here, I'm gonna need to get outta the street, then outta the cab, then outta your house, then off your roof, then outta the sky, then outta my hair, right outta my hair ... get me outta hair!"

As his whisper rose to a scream, I pulled his spindly albino body off me and flung him against the front window. He hit with a gray-blooded splat.

"What the hell was that?" hollered the cashier, already holding the first deer upside down and shaking him.

"I d-don't h-have m-money, I n-need m-money," said the jostling beast.

I wanted to help the cashier, so I went over and offered to hold the thing down, but the guy only glared at me.

"There are no pets allowed in the laundromat," he said.

"These aren't my pets. They followed me. The little sons of bitches followed me," I said.

"I called 9-1-1," said an old woman, pulling a toddler closer and joining the cashier in his glare. Outside, I noticed the red flash of police cruisers and heard the injured animal moaning in front of the cracked glass. Between the cops, the cashier, the grannies, and the little peckerhead deer, I could see they were going to make a monster out of me. I had no choice but to bolt for the back door.

At least the civilians were afraid to pursue. I emerged in a slabstone courtyard, the type a restaurant could have made a back patio out of. A steel fence stood at the far end, top-lined with razor wire. Behind a clump of smog-withered maple trees, I heard some sounds, one obviously a woman, a woman saying "Yes" like she meant it. The other was a series of short snorts and what might have been hooves scraping stone. I bolted for the fence.

Scaling it was easy enough, but in my first attempt, I didn't have enough momentum to slip between the spiraling steel blades. Instead, I hung from a square bar in a frozen chin-up.

"I see you spying up there," called D-Deer from where he was sitting on a stump, smoking a fresh cigarette.

"Get over here, let me stand on your shoulders," I yelled back.

"What the hell for? Hey, stop that baby," he said to the girl as she sat up, red hair frazzled, eyes still hungry, hands reaching around to coax him back down. "Stop that. And you, over by the fence, it's gonna take more than chin-ups to impress a lady who just got the deep dip from D-Deer!"

He was sticking out his chest again and flexing his muscles, but stopped short when he was hit by a speeding blob of gray fur.

"I goooootttttahh get ououououtta heeeere!!!" screamed the fur ball as it dashed in furious circles trailed by four burly cops.

I tried to hang on, tried to pull with my weakening grip, tried to remember that there was a time when I could go home to my fiancée and bitch about the office, to remember that the office wasn't so bad and there was no need to have told a financial analyst to get his mangy ass out of my cubicle; no need to have told my manager, when he asked about it, that the analyst's ass really was mangy, and maybe he should go rub his nose in it to see that I was right. I had to hang on to the possibility that the things I had before could come back again.

I felt a cop's hands on my boot, pulling me down. "Let go. You're resisting arrest."

"No, you let go. Please, you let go, just let me go over this fuckin' fence. I don't even need to go to the hospital, nothing, just let me run and I swear I'll be better, I'll be better ..."

He released his grip, giving the gentle method a try. "Son, you're gonna add more charges onto an already long list. It may not seem like it now, but down the road you'll be kicking yourself for that extra four years."

I kicked him in the face. "Arrest the deer! Arrest the damn deer! They're the ones who damaged the property! They're not with me! That one with the diamonds is a rapist! Get him!"

But they were pulling me in earnest now, four of them linking arms. It was my pair of locked elbows against their foursome of uniform and torso. Blood blurred my vision and dripped down my forehead with a salty sting from where the razors scraped my scalp. Here in this final heart-thumping trance, it wasn't the cops' strength or even the prods of the deer that made me let go. It was a crimson vision of Angela, my fiancée, the one who I once called the most important in the world, the dearest person in my life. It was her throwing me out of our apartment, telling me I had no right to quit my job, not when I was only halfway through paying her back for the last six-month bout of unemployment ... and that tacked on to the three month stint before that, during which time we waited for blood tests because of the prostitute thing, and then there was the waitress ... was that after the landlord came pounding on the door? I couldn't remember. Somewhere in there I lost a check, and they weren't easy to replace.

**

Of course they did arrest the deer, too. All of them. They brought us to a cement cell painted bright white with tissue-paper sheets on the bed. The cop that I kicked gave me one last jab in the ribs, broke some I think, as he handed me over to the staff at the facility.

"You yuppie fucks always get the cush cells," he barked.

The next man I saw wasn't much for conversation; he just put the needle in me and said that if I was good, it'd be pills next time. I tried to tell him it was the deer he needed to be shooting up, especially the twitchy little gray one who was trying to chew a rat hole behind the toilet.

But they did seem to mellow out after an hour or so, and even D-Deer was yawning through his distress.

"Not gonna find much pussy in here," he said. "Might as well sleep."

"At least it's free," said the first deer, who then laid down and let his day-old sweat fill our confines with a belly-twisting stench.

The walls, the ceiling, the windowless door—I knew all of them were promising pain to come. And it was going to belong to all of us, these cellmates of mine, so close, so heavy and so warm. I lost track of time in this place, failing to emerge for anything the ones on the outside tried to get me to do. Didn't they understand that the one time I'd brought someone in close, really close, I'd failed to put her needs before mine? They were fools, but they insisted on trying. One day they even said I had a special visitor—this pretty, tan young woman with a cloth bag on her arm. She was all smiley and touching my hand. Then, when she said my name, I remembered hers—Montana, the hippy girl who owned the boutique, the one who'd put me up the night before the deer attacked.

And it turned out they were right about this visitor being special, because she didn't try to get me to talk about anyone or anything that wasn't true. Instead, she showed me her new artwork, pulled clothes from the bag that she was making and selling. At last she produced a pair of ink-covered tights, ink splattered in the shapes of antlers and hooves. I could see she knew the difference between what was real and what was not, and so I forgave her when she said that if I ever felt better, I could get a job helping in her shop.

"Until then," she said, "take these tights. And hold on to them this time."

"I will," I said, avoiding her kiss on the cheek and going back to my mattress. It was covered in mounds of musky fur and loaded with three pairs of empty eyes that stared hazy stares. I lay down on that mattress, no longer anxious about what I had before, because I realized here that I was already at rest in the arms of my deer.

The Jersey Devil

BY MIKE SEGRETTO

"Hey, kids. Are you ready to have fun?"

Lee Ronnie Lee hiked up his oversized, polka-dotted trousers and scratched his ass.

"Yeah!"

"I can't hear you."

Asking the preceding question was just part of his shtick. In actuality, he could hear the shrieking coven of sugar-buzzed 7-year-olds perfectly well. Furthermore, if he had his way, none of them would be remotely audible and only a handful of them would be alive. Still, he had a job to do, and the kids replied on cue with the eardrum-raping volume of a herd of chimpanzees in labor.

"YEAH!"

Lee Ronnie Lee sighed and mustered every lingering bit of his energy to continue on. "Great. My name is Spanky the Clown, and I'm here to entertain you guys. Got it?"

He opened a box adorned with multi-colored question marks, which he called his "Trunk O' Tricks," and pulled out a boom box. Lee Ronnie hit the 'play' button on the tape player and a mechanized drumbeat tinnily creaked out of the one working speaker. He half-heartedly chanted along with the rhythm.

"I'm Spanky the Clown and I'm here to say,
Gonna rock you kids in a bodacious way.
I'm the clowningest clown that you ever seen,
Got a seltzer-squirtin' flower and an M-16.
Y'all will love it when I tell my jokes
You'll be laughin' yourselves silly 'til you drop and croak
And when I bust open my 'Trunk O' Tricks'
Each one of you be howlin', 'Aww, man, that's sick!'
When the party is pumpin', gonna rock the floor
Make y'all start laughin' till ya' can't laugh no more
And when the puns be rollin', ya' gonna lose control
Cause I got more soul than Dr. Scholl ... *Break it down!*"

As Lee Ronnie Lee jerked into an arrhythmic jig, the kids simply glared at him in stunned silence. The music petered out. His dance ended shortly thereafter. He bent over to hit the stop button on the stereo before turning back to face the crowd.

"Alright, which one of you is the birthday girl?"

"Go on, Kristy." The mother of a little girl with long braids nudged her daughter. The tyke reluctantly rose to join Lee Ronnie by the backyard fence. She meekly stood next to him, her eyes fixed on her penny loafers.

"Well, Kristy, is it?"

"Uh huh."

"You ready to party, Kristy?"

"I dunno."

Lee Ronnie Lee crouched down to meet the girl face to face, nearly nuzzling her with his bulbous, rubber nose. He lowered his voice to chat privately with the timid little thing. "What's the matter there, Kristy? You don't look like you're having much fun."

"I don't like clowns."

"Then why the fuck did your mom hire one for your party?"

Kristy gazed at Lee Ronnie for several interminable seconds. Then she expelled a scream that nearly peeled the grease paint from his face.

"MOOOOOOOOOOOM! SPANKY THE CLOWN SAID A BAD WORD!"

"Take it easy, kid," he peeped out of the corner of his mouth.

"What?" Kristy's mother was confused and not remotely amused.

"HE SAID THE 'FUCK' WORD!"

All the kids detonated into manic laughter as Kristy's mom—as well as all the other moms at the party—marched toward Lee Ronnie Lee.

"Where do you get off using that kind of language around my daughter?" Kristy's mom bellowed.

"She's lying, lady. I didn't say any bad words. I'm a professional." Lee Ronnie honked his nose to punctuate his point.

"My daughter does not lie! She's a good girl."

"Good girl? Did you hear the mouth on that kid? She curses like a goddamned longshoreman."

"I want you off my property now."

"That's cool, lady. Just get me my fifty bucks and I'll be on my way."

"Are you insane? I'm not paying you a dime."

Lee Ronnie Lee yanked off his rubber nose to indicate he meant business. "Are you fucking joking? I got all dressed up and put on my make up and all that shit, and you're not even gonna pay me? What kind of clip joint is this?"

"Madge, call the police," Kristy's mom shouted back to one of the other mothers.

"Alright, alright, you goddamn welcher. I'm out of here." Lee Ronnie Lee stopped and sneered down at Kristy. "Happy birthday, punk. I hope you get cancer." He packed up his Trunk O' Tricks and slinked off to his 1982 Honda Prelude.

***

A mile away at The Rubber Nipple on the Jersey Turnpike, several of Lee Ronnie Lee's fellow birthday-party clowns were unwinding after a grueling afternoon of prancing in front of unappreciative toddlers. At The Rubber Nipple, they could disappear into the crowd, no longer having to humiliate themselves on center stage. As per the sacred "Party Clown's Code," everyone referred to each other by their performing handles and rarely shared personal information about themselves. The sole concern of the patrons of The Rubber Nipple was to forget about their miserable existences by drinking themselves into blind stupors while ogling strippers. Of course, they probably would have done a far better job of forgetting their existences had they patronized a strip club where the dancers didn't dress like clowns.

Lee Ronnie Lee moped to the bar and sat next to Chuck Chuckles, who had spent the better part of the morning being pelted by fawn droppings at a petting zoo.

"What gives, Spanky?" Chuck marveled. "They're already petting goats. Why the hell do they need a clown on top of that?"

"Beats the dick out of me, Chuck. This whole business is a mystery to me. To be honest with you, I don't even understand what's so hilarious about rainbow wigs and giant shoes. I guess kids will just laugh at anything. Fucking idiots."

"So, why do you do it?"

"The money, Chuck. Just for the money. I don't plan on being a party clown for the rest of my life. I have, you know, artistic aspirations."

Chuck Chuckles momentarily zoned out, mesmerized by a stripper named Spitzolina who was currently kneeling before him on the bar. She twirled her rainbow tassels in perfect sync with Gary Lewis and the Playboys' "Everybody Loves a Clown" as it blared out of the sound system.

"Chuck? You listening?"

"Oh, yeah. Artistic aspirations." Chuck wiped a dab of spittle from his lower lip with the back of his hand and took a sip of J&B. "What kind of artistic aspirations?"

"Funny you should ask that, my friend." Lee Ronnie Lee's voice suddenly acquired a distinct tinge of pride. "I am going to be a filmmaker. All I need is enough cash to get started."

"Yeah? How much does it cost to make a movie?"

"Well, I'm not 100% sure, but I think it takes a lot. Like $500 or so."

"Shit. That's a lot of money, man." Chuck Chuckles took another sip and directed his attention back to Spitzolina who was now blowing up balloons with her vagina and twisting them into animal shapes. "That's some act, eh, Spanky?"

"Yeah, $500. I'm gonna get it someday, and then I can make my very own picture."

Chuck focused back on his peer. "So, what kind of picture are you gonna make? One of them political action movies?"

"No, I'm making a thriller. I got the script written and everything. It's gonna be loaded with high-tech special effects and big Hollywood stars and thrills and suspense and all that crap."

"That sounds terrific, Spanky. What are you gonna call it?"

"*Mania 2: One Million and One Murders*."

"What about *Mania 1*?"

"Sequels always do better at the box office, so I'm skipping *Mania 1*."

"That's pretty smart. Sounds like you got it all figured out."

"I sure do. My girlfriend Darla is gonna star as Jenny Bricket the voluptuous park ranger at Camp Hackenhurl, which is where teenage girls are being mysteriously chainsawed by a serial mani-ac. I been studying all the movies by the great masters of sus-pense; all the geniuses like Alfred Hitchcock, Roman Polanski, Mischu Lambretta ..."

"Mischu who? I ain't never heard of him."

"You never heard of Mischu Lambretta? Man, you gotta get out to the cinema more often, Chuckles. Mischu Lambretta is only the original Italian master of splatter. He practically invented film violence in the '60s with classics like *The Disembowelers* and *Haiku: Finger of Death*."

"Never seen 'em. He making many pictures these days?"

"Well, in the mid-'60s he was forced into exile when he was accused of being involved with an English street gang that mur-dered some has-been actor. Last I heard, Mischu was living in Vietnam making blenema movies."

Chuckles took a pull off his J&B and squinted at Lee Ronnie. "Blenema? What's that?"

"It's this exotic sex practice they have in the Orient. They get these 13-year-old boys, strip 'em naked, and attach high-powered industrial wet-dry vacs to their penises. The vacuums suck so hard that they actually pull matter from the anus through the urethra causing the boys to ejaculate feces. They call that 'fejaculating'."

"Jesus Christ. That's a blenema, eh?"

"Yeah, the name is sort of shorthand for a blow job/enema,

although it goes by all sorts of names: the front-door colonic, the diddy dump, the Charlie Brown ..."

"Charlie Brown? I don't get it."

"You know ... 'Charlie'... Vietnam. Get it?"

"Oh yeah." Chuckles took another sip of his drink. "Isn't that kind of racist, though?"

"I don't think people who like to watch 13-year-old boys blast shit out of their pee-holes are usually that culturally sensitive."

"Gotcha. So your movie is gonna be one of them blenema movies, is it?"

"No, no, no. That's just what I hear Mischu Lambretta is doing these days. My movie isn't gonna be about sex, you see. It's about violence. It's gonna usher in a whole new era of splatter, and I bet Mischu Lambretta will even be able to return from Vietnam so that he can quit making that exploitative crap and start making movies like *Storm Trooper Blood Orgy* again."

"That's a hell of a dream, Spanky." As Spitzolina handed him a balloon twisted into the shape of an ocelot that happened to have her phone number scrawled on it in black magic marker, Chuck Chuckles was now detached from his conversation with Lee Ronnie Lee for good.

"I know it is, Chuck. Now I just gotta figure out where I'm gonna get $500. I'd sell my soul for that kinda scratch."

***

As the hours passed, Lee Ronnie Lee faded further and further into the shadowy background of The Rubber Nipple. While his peers wasted the night getting blitzed and tossing their hard-earned dollars at girls with names like Amber and Bubbles, Lee Ronnie was hunched behind a table, inhaling Lucky Strike after

Lucky Strike, futilely devising ways that he might come into $500.

"What's the matter, poopsy? You don't look like you're having much fun." The breathy voice drew Lee Ronnie out of his isolated scheming.

"Hey, baby! You off work yet? How much you pull in tonight?"

Darla Bonjour thrust out her lower lip in an over-exaggerated pout. "Not much, Lee Ronnie baby. Just $20 and I had to let Colonel Pom-Pom paw me for two hours to get it."

"Pom-Pom—that hack. He's still using jokes he stole from Bozo thirty years ago. You believe that shit, Darla?"

Darla chirped a vacuous giggle. "I don't know. I'm just an actress." She twirled her platinum curls with a finger so elegantly slim that it seemed completely out of place on a body that supported such a bountifully buxom bust.

Lee Ronnie pulled Darla onto his lap. "That's right, baby. Best damn actress in this goddamn city. And you know what?"

Darla threw her arms around her lover's neck and gazed into his pink, watery eyes. "What?"

"I'm gonna make you a star. Just you wait, baby. You're gonna be the biggest star since Pia Zadora."

"Oh, Lee Ronnie!"

Lee Ronnie exhaled a cloud of cigarette smoke and Darla lunged in for a deep, damp, loving kiss. For just a moment, Lee Ronnie Lee almost felt content.

When they disengaged from their lip lock, he peered down at the table. "Where the hell did that come from?"

Darla craned her neck. "I don't know."

On the table sat a tiny box adorned with question marks. It looked not unlike a dwarf cousin of the Trunk O' Tricks. However, this box had a crank on its front panel.

"Oh, Lee Ronnie, wind it up! I simply adore music boxes!"

Darla urged.

"Well, I guess I ain't got nothing to lose." Lee Ronnie Lee snubbed out his butt in the ashtray and picked up the little box. He cautiously rotated the crank as a hauntingly rickety rendition of AC/DC's "Hell's Bells" emanated from the mystery box. Just as the song came to the point where Brian Johnson would have screamed, "I got my bell, I'm gonna take you to hell / I'm gonna get ya', Satan get ya'," the top of the box popped like a champagne cork, and a doll with a hooked chin, a hooked nose, and a jester's cap bounced forward violently. In its tiny ceramic hands, it held an envelope.

"Why, Lee Ronnie Lee, that envelope has your name on it! It says, 'Lee Ronnie Lee'!"

With a trembling hand, he reached forward and clutched the envelope, which the doll was not quick to give up. Lee Ronnie was more than a little disturbed by the doll's strength and resolve, but after some yanking and struggling, he freed the envelope from its guardian.

"Open it up, Lee Ronnie!"

He ran his finger through the fold, giving himself a nasty paper cut in the process.

"Oh, honey, you're bleeding!"

As Darla poked her paramour's bloody finger into her mouth, sucking it like a baby lamb with a pacifier, Lee Ronnie used his free hand to snatch the note from the envelope. He then read it aloud.

"When life is hard and beats you down
And you feel a fool ... or worse ... a clown
And all your dreams are nowhere near
The path to them may soon a-pier.
For way down South, in just an hour

Your time will come; you'll get your power
Since without five-hundred you're sure to snap
You'd be advised to seek The Gap."

Lee Ronnie Lee paused and pondered, piecing the puzzling poem together in his pallid pate.

"That sure is a pretty song, Lee Ronnie," Darla cooed. "You want to go home and screw our brains out?"

Lee Ronnie Lee, however, was lost in deep reflection, murmuring to himself all the while. "A-pier. A-pier. I don't think that's how that word is spelled. Must be a clue. A-pier. Hmmm. Down South. South. Pier. A pier down South. Where is there a pier down South?"

"I don't know, lover. China?"

Lee Ronnie reread the poem silently to himself, moving his lips along as he digested each word. "That's funny. The words 'South' and 'The Gap' are capitalized. Like they're specific places." With that, Lee Ronnie Lee jolted forward, toppling Darla to the floor of The Rubber Nipple. "Wait a minute, Darla. The pier down at South Street Seaport over the turnpike in New York City! I think there's a Gap store down there! You know, where they sell reasonably affordable but conservatively stylish clothing for the conventionally-minded young adult! I think the note is telling me to go there in an hour. It also mentions the number 'five-hundred!' Darla, baby, I gotta get down to that Gap on the pier of the South Street Seaport in an hour. I think this just might be the break we been waiting for!"

"That's wonderful, sweetie! Now can you help me up? I think I fell in some spooge."

***

Lee Ronnie Lee revved the engine of his Honda as hard as the bitty thing could rev. There was little time to spare, as the South Street Seaport in New York City was quite a distance from Newark. Lee Ronnie raced down the Jersey Turnpike with little regard for traffic cops, pushing his tiny vehicle to chassis-rattling speeds of 48-miles an hour. Hitting a nasty patch of late-day traffic, he slyly pulled up onto the median and raced on.

He arrived in the southernmost tip of Manhattan just as the sun sank behind the steely skyline, the seaport now illuminated by the soft glow of street lamps. Long shadows stretched across the pier like the swiping paws of panthers. Even though Lee Ronnie was of singular mind, he could not help but take notice of the foreboding chill whisking through the evening, and he pulled his yellow and pink polka-dot overcoat around himself just a little tighter.

The warm fluorescent lights glowing from within The Gap did not provide any respite from the ominous sensation wrapping around Lee Ronnie Lee like a death shroud, but he moved on in spite of his apprehension. If there was any truth to the note he'd received, then he would be foolish to succumb to irrational trepidation. Perhaps an anonymous zillionaire in the Rubber Nipple had overheard his conversation with Chuck Chuckles and was interested in financing his film. But why would such a person lead him to The Gap?

"Excuse me, sir, but you look like you could use some khaki cargo pants."

Lee Ronnie Lee stopped pretending to browse through Gap Maternity dresses and looked up to see a woman peering at him from over the rack. She was stunningly striking with her green, feline eyes and alabaster skin disrupted only by a perfectly placed beauty mark just over the corner of her sly, red lips. Her blue-black hair was shaped into a severe Bettie Page cut. She exuded intimidating confidence even though her curvaceous figure was rather schlubbily garbed in a pair of pleated slacks and a dingy, red Gap-associate vest, no doubt worn by many a chirpy clerk before her.

"Sorry, sister," Lee Ronnie responded. "I'm meeting someone here."

"You sure I can't interest you in some cargo pants? I think I have just the right size for you."

"Pffft," he scoffed. "How could you possibly know my size? You trying to convince me you're some sort of magician?"

"Oh, I don't know," she purred coyly. "You just look to me like you might be a ... *large*." A heart-spanking thunderclap exploded just as the woman revealed Lee Ronnie Lee's exact pants size.

"H-h-how did you know that I'm a l-large?" he stammered.

"Oh, I don't know, Mr. Lee." She vanished and reappeared behind him suddenly, leaning over his shoulder to whisper in his ear confidentially. "Perhaps it is because ... *I'm the Devil*."

"Shit, I don't believe in any devils." His attempt to mask his terror was entirely unconvincing. "If you're the Devil, what are you doing working at The Gap?"

"Where else would the Devil work, Mr. Lee?"

She had a point. The Devil slipped her snaky fingers into Lee Ronnie Lee's hand and led him to the front doors of The Gap.

"Hey, Sheila!" shouted Rusty the store manager as he barreled into the Devil's path. "Where the heck do you think you're going? You still have an hour left on your shift."

The Devil waved her hand before the manager's face, and with chilling control murmured, "I am going for a cigarette break, Rusty."

Rusty's beady eyes glazed over. His tubby body jolted into paralytic rigidity. "You. Are. Going. For. A. Cigarette. Break," he droned.

"That's a good little manager, Rusty." The Devil patted Rusty's head as though he were a well-tamed pup and resumed walking to the door.

Lee Ronnie Lee remained frozen in the store, marveling at Rusty's catatonia.

"You coming or not?" the Devil prodded.

"Ummm, yeah." Lee Ronnie shook himself out of his fascination and passed into the night to converse with the Princess of Darkness.

The Devil was already half finished with her Pall Mall when Lee Ronnie stumbled onto the sidewalk. She stood with her back against the store and one of her New Balance-clad feet propped up on the wall behind her.

"Cigarette, Mr. Lee?"

"Hell yes," he quaked.

The Devil snapped her fingers, and with alarming immediacy, a lit cigarette popped straight out of the ether and in between Lee Ronnie's quivering lips.

"So, I understand you have aspirations in the cinema, Mr. Lee."

"How did you know that?"

The Devil rolled her eyes and pointed toward the nametag on her Gap vest. Lee Ronnie bent down to peruse the tag.

"*Sheila*," he read.

"Oops." The Devil snapped her fingers again, and the name on her tag suddenly morphed into *The Devil*. "I just go by the name "Sheila" when I'm working. No one would hire me if they knew my name was actually Lucifer, Beelzebub, Old Scratch, Mephistopheles, el Diablo, Belial, Satan ... the Devil."

"Probably couldn't fit all of that onto a name tag, anyways."

"REGARDLESS!" The Devil's mighty shout was punctuated with another deafening detonation of thunder, and Lee Ronnie cowered accordingly. He fell to his knees and shielded his eyes from the demonic overlord, who was lighting up another Pall Mall. "So, I received word that you are in need of $500. Am I correct?"

"Ummm, well, yes, but when I said I'd sell my soul for that money, I just meant it as a sort of figure of speech. I didn't actually mean, well, you know ..."

The Devil emitted a mildly irritated sigh. "Oh, please. What do you think this is? A friggin' Betty Boop cartoon? These days, every doucheroo who has his eyes on government office or Paris Hilton's snatch is ready to cough up his soul. I have more souls than I know what to do with, and frankly, I'm running out of room. No. What I want is much simpler. I'd like a role in your movie."

"Really?"

"Yeah. Frankly, I'm tired of hawking crappy polo shirts and capri pants at The Gap. Just because I'm the Devil, doesn't mean I don't have an artistic side to express. Hence, I would like to play the lead role in your movie."

"Hmmm. Well, you see," Lee Ronnie stumbled, "thing is, I kinda already promised that part to my girlfriend."

"Ahhh, yes. The bimbo who wipes her fanny against clown crotches for a few bucks to keep her in peroxide and spandex. I'm aware of her. Well, you're just going to have to give her another part."

"Well ..."

***

"You what?" When enraged, Darla's pipsqueak voice took on the piercing quality of an air horn loaded with helium. "You gave away my part to some ... some ... pleated pants-wearing stock girl?"

"The Devil, baby," Lee Ronnie corrected. "She's the Devil, and this is the only way I'm gonna get this picture made. I still have a pretty decent part for you as Nurse Bombana the killer's final victim."

"Are you kiddin'?" she squawked. "I gotta go from the star of this picture to some chainsawed tart?"

"No, honey, no. She doesn't get killed with the chainsaw. In fact, I rewrote the script a little to give you a real flashy send off. Trust me. This is the kind of part that makes careers."

"I dunno."

"I'm serious, baby! Once I get this one made, you're gonna star as the Den Mother in *Mania 3: The Slicing of Pack 604*. I promise. Check it out." Lee Ronnie pulled five crisp one-hundred dollar bills from his pocket. He waved the bills under Darla's crinkling nose. They smelled faintly of sulfur.

"You're a real turd. You know that?" She half-heartedly attempted to repress the smile that was tickling onto her lips.

Lee Ronnie grinned and grabbed his girl. "I knew you'd come around, doll face."

***

Despite Darla's reluctance regarding her newly diminished role in the film, Lee Ronnie soldiered on. After all, one of the duties of an auteur was to manage the inflated egos of his cast. And as he soon learned, an ornery starlet was the least of his concerns; for you see, $500 is hardly enough money to rent a movie camera for a week, let alone finance an entire motion picture.

So, Lee Ronnie Lee began making cuts. Instead of shooting the film on location in Canada, as he'd originally planned, he would film it locally on a playground in Hackensack. Instead of casting one of his top picks to play the role of the chainsaw-wielding maniac, he would be playing the part himself in lieu of Keanu Reeves, Brad Pitt, or the guy who played Fez on *That 70s Show*. He decided to replace the ravenous grizzly bear sequence with one involving a far less costly donkey. He switched from celluloid to video, a painful move, which he felt undercut a great deal of his artistic vision. Worse yet, all of the elaborate special effects he'd mapped out for the film would clearly be impossible to achieve on such a limited budget. There was only one thing he could do.

"I'm gonna need more money."

"Oh no," the Devil snapped as she stocked the men's department with boxer shorts decorated with a pattern depicting a fey sailor using a chorizo as a golf club. "A deal is a deal, clowny boy."

"But there's no way I'm gonna make this picture with five hundred lousy bucks!"

"Sorry. That's not my problem, Ace. Furthermore, I already gave Rusty my two week's notice, so if you don't figure out how to get this movie made, I'm going to be unemployed. The Devil *cannot* be unemployed. How would that look to the sniveling masses? No siree. Either you make this movie or I'm gonna have to take your soul."

"But that wasn't part of the deal!"

"Neither was this bullshit about needing more money."

"But you said you didn't need any more souls."

"I don't, but there has to be some kind of price. Maybe I'll use it as a pommel horse or something. The Devil's gotta stay fit, you know."

Lee Ronnie Lee fell to his knees in desperation. "What am I going to do?" he mused aloud. "If I'd known that a deal with the Devil might have a downside, I never would've bothered in the first place!"

"Off the floor," the Devil peeped surreptitiously, giving Lee

Ronnie a light kick in the butt. "You trying to get me fired?"

"Sorry." Lee Ronnie Lee got to his feet before Rusty caught sight of his performance. "I just wish ..."

"Yes?" The Devil arched an eyebrow sexily.

"... I wish I could talk to someone who knows how to make a high-quality gore film on a reserved budget."

"Oh, alright."

The Devil led Lee Ronnie outside for another "cigarette break." But instead of firing up one of her Pall Malls, she set her eyes ablaze, cocked a hip, and snapped her fingers. As though the atmosphere were a well-swelled pimple just pinched, a swarthy little Italian man popped into place as though he were the pus.

"Mischu Lambretta!" Lee Ronnie Lee gasped.

"Hey, what's-a all this?" Though Lambretta must have been well into his seventies, he still had a head of thick, black hair and relatively taut, thoroughly-tanned skin. He wore a black turtleneck sweater and impenetrably dark shades, which he lowered only to take a gander at the Devil with his frog-like eyes. "Oh, it's you!"

"Hey, Mischu," she replied.

"You know each other?" Lee Ronnie asked.

"Oh yes! She give me my start making picture," Lambretta replied in his thick Tuscan twang.

"So, I'm not your first filmmaker?"

"You kidding, Spanky?" The Devil guffawed. "How do you think James Cameron got so big? Trust me, *Titanic* didn't become such a smash hit because people were genuinely dying to line up for a sappy, twelve-hour disaster film starring that retarded blonde girl from *What's Eating Gilbert Grape*."

"That makes a lot of sense."

"Alright," the Devil resumed. "So, you wanted to talk to an expert. Well, I got you an expert."

"Yes," Lambretta concurred proudly. "Mischu an expert. I no make a film like *They Stabbed Lincoln's Brain* because I some kind of amateur."

"Ok then," Lee Ronnie Lee began. "So, how do I make a feature film on a budget of $500?"

"Hmmm." Lambretta stroked his chin thoughtfully for several moments. "Well, I say you do what Mischu do."

"You mean I should make a blenema movie?"

"What blenema movie? Mischu no make no blenema movie."

"You know, you really can't make someone squirt crap out of their hoo-ha," the Devil explained. "Believe me, I've tried many, many times, and let me tell you, Jesus was *not* amused."

"So, it was all just a rumor?" Lee Ronnie asked.

"Yes, yes. Ugly rumor." Lambretta gesticulated madly as he spoke. "Mischu no make movie like that. He just make the snuff film."

"You mean like that one with Kate Moss in the recording studio?"

"No, no, no. Different kind of snuff. Mischu make movie where the people get killed for real. Very unexpensive to make. Make my first one in 1960s where crazy English actor kill old man by biting his neck off. After that, Mischu have to leave Europe because they no like the kill movie there. He go to Vietnam. Vietnam very crazy at that time. They burn down Mischu's village, but I record it all on the videotape and sell it to some Vietcong for a hog. That hog make Mischu a very rich man. After that, I never go back to old way of making film. After that, Mischu make the snuff all the time."

"So, you're saying I have to kill someone?"

"It the only way. Killing people is very cheap, you know. All you need these day is camcorder and VHS tape and somebody to kill. Now Mischu got to go. He filming a family of water-chestnut farmers getting eaten by a sand shark in an hour. Bye bye." With a bubble-busting *POP*! Lambretta disappeared.

"But who?" Lee Ronnie Lee was at a loss. "Who do I kill?"

"Well," the Devil interjected, "there's always my co-star. You know ... the pinhead."

"You're not suggesting I kill my girlfriend, are you?"

"Think of it as a career move, Mr. Lee."

***

The shoot had been going extraordinarily well. In spite of Lee Ronnie Lee's limited fiscal resources, he still managed to shoot some exquisite exteriors along the smokestack-strewn Jersey Turnpike and outside the historic fat-rendering plants of Secaucus. Although Darla remained noticeably cool toward her beau during the shoot, as she was still smarting from losing the plum role of Jenny Bricket to the Devil, she still drew upon all of her dramatic skills during her scenes. Lee got some particularly enticing footage of Darla sunbathing in nothing more than a rice paper thong and a coconut bra on the Jersey shore during the "Satanic Clambake" sequence.

Better yet, the Devil proved to be a formidable acting talent, not unlike a young Shelly Winters without the excess fattage. The Devil's screen presence—her reactions, her dialogue readings, her ability to switch on emotion as naturally as one might blow one's nose—was positive proof that all those years of orchestrating man's inhumanity to man and checking out customers at The Gap were, indeed, years that could have been better spent in front of a camera. All in all, the film was coming together so smashingly that Lee Ronnie had to admit that the Devil had made good on her word.

Still, he was in no rush to shoot one particular scene—biding his time in the hope that the Devil might have a change of heart.

But whenever he broached the subject with her, she would always flash him the same incredulous look and simply reiterate, "Dude, I'm the fucking Devil."

With 462 minutes of footage in the can, there was no more delaying the inevitable.

"Ok, Darla." Lee Ronnie Lee wrung his sweaty palms together. "This is your big scene."

Darla sat in a folding chair, filing her nails. Without even looking up at the director, she croaked, "Well, it's about time."

Not wishing to intensify the tensions on set—which happened to be his basement apartment in his mom's Monmouth home—Lee Ronnie ignored Darla's caustic tone, clapped his hands enthusiastically, and shouted, "Ok, let's see that donkey!"

The door at the top of the stairs swung open, and the Devil led a rather large, rather malodorous donkey down on a leash. To approximate the appearance of the grizzly bear for which the donkey was standing in, Lee Ronnie had draped the beast with a few old 'coonskin coats he'd unearthed in the attic, most likely leftovers from his mother's flapper days during the '20s.

The Devil brought the donkey to the center of the room and situated it over a wooden bucket. She stepped into the shadows. She smiled.

After applying the final touches of his clown makeup, Lee Ronnie walked over to Darla. He swallowed hard. His mouth was drier than Joe Franklin.

"Alright, baby," he began with a quaver in his voice. "This is it. So, in this scene, you're attending to the latest victims of the chainsaw-wielding maniac—that's me. You need to get them some milk. That's when you see a grizzly bear—that's the donkey—and you mistake it for a cow. So, you get down beneath it and start milking it. That's when I sneak up behind you—or rather the maniac sneaks up behind you, and he bludgeons you to death with a giant kiel-basa."

Darla frowned at Lee Ronnie. "So, you're gonna hit me with a kielbasa? Isn't that going to muss my hair?"

"Don't worry about it, doll. Kielbasas are soft. Your hair won't feel a thing."

"Alright," she reluctantly agreed. "If you say so."

Lee Ronnie choked back a tear. "That's a good girl."

Now, what Lee Ronnie Lee failed to tell Darla Bonjour was that he had left the giant kielbasa in question in his mother's freezer overnight, during which time it chilled from a harmless, tasty Polish sausage into a rock hard, frosty instrument of death.

"Alright," he announced. "We're gonna shoot this." As Lee Ronnie was to be part of the scene, he had to relinquish camera duties to the Devil, who was only too happy to be on the business end of the eyepiece for this particular scene.

From out of frame, Lee Ronnie shouted, "Ok, Devil ... roll it!"

The Devil clicked on the video camera.

"And ... action, Darla!"

Darla plopped down on a small metal stool beside the donkey. Then she looked directly into the camera lens and bellowed her lines with the fluidity of a brain-damaged six-year-old reading aloud from *Ulysses*.

"Oh, I am sure worried about those victims of the maniac! How could anyone be so maniacal?" She cocked her head stiffly toward the donkey. "Oh, look! It is a cow! From this cow, I shall get milk for the maniac's victims, so they will be able to rebuild their strength with coffee and breakfast cereal!"

Darla looked back at Lee Ronnie, not quite sure what to do next. He responded by miming milking motions in the air with his hands.

Darla braced herself. She rubbed her hands together vigorously to warm them. The donkey pivoted its 'coonskin draped head toward her, uncertain of what she planned to do. She paused. She breathed deeply. She asked herself, "What would Meryl Streep do in this situation?" She answered herself, "She'd be a professional. Meryl Streep would milk the donkey." So, with only one option present, Darla rolled up her sleeves and began milking the donkey.*

"Boy!" she bellowed. "This cow sure does like to be milked!" She turned around and winked at the camera.

Meanwhile, Lee Ronnie Lee stood off-camera. His back hunched. His face drenched in perspiration. His heart throbbing against his chest fiercely. His stomach twisting and tightening like the knot at the end of a noose. He took the great, frozen kielbasa in his hands and gave the Devil one last pleading glance. She nodded her head toward Darla agitatedly. He had no choice.

Darla repeated Lee Ronnie's cue with even greater volume. "I SAID THIS COW SURE DOES LIKE TO BE MILKED!!"

Mopping his sweat-drenched brow with his forearm, Lee Ronnie Lee steeled himself. He crept up behind Darla, who was still cheerfully milking the donkey. The creature's eyes rolled back in its head with pleasure.

Lee Ronnie raised the frozen kielbasa over his head. His hands shook with such crazed fervor he could hardly keep it still

Darla milked on.

The Devil came in for a tight close-up of her smiling face.

The donkey released a guttural groan.

The tension in the room was thicker than a thunderous thigh.

The Devil's face flushed red. She gripped the camera so tightly that she threatened to crush it between her palms. "NOW!" she shrieked.

* (note to reader: Darla is now jerking the donkey off to hilariously comedic effect.)

Just as Lee Ronnie Lee shifted to drop the massive, hardened sausage upon his darling's skull, the donkey caught sight of what was about to happen. Not about to have the lady who was stroking him into ecstasy murdered before she'd "finished the job," the donkey bucked. Darla tumbled off her stool spastically, careening into Lee Ronnie. He spiraled uncontrollably, round and round and round the room in dizzy rings, finally collapsing onto his hands and knees, back to back with the snarling, blue-balled beast. The donkey furiously back-kicked Lee Ronnie Lee with such animal force that it actually pushed his colon through the front of his body, where it tore through his urethra, causing him to fejaculate violently all over the basement of his mother's house.

As Lee Ronnie Lee gasped his final breath and slumped lifelessly to the shit-stained shag carpet, the Devil lowered the camera, gazing in sheer astonishment. "Well, how about that? It is possible after all!"

Unable to look away from the gruesome scene—a scene destined to become a genuine classic of the cinema—the Devil reflexively lit a Pall Mall. She held out the pack to Darla. With her face devoid of color, the aspiring starlet took the Black Angel's final cigarette and placed it between her pouty lips.

"So, are you really the Devil?" Darla asked.

"Uh huh," the Devil grunted, still struggling to wrap her head around what she'd just witnessed.

"You think you could make me a star?"

"Just a sec, dear." The Devil snapped out of her stupor, rushed up the stairs, and called behind herself, "I really have to see if I can get Jesus on the phone."

The Left Side

BY WARD CROCKETT

So, you wanna hear about ol' Hackett and the doll necklace, eh? Sure you do. You wanna know how I brought down Opie and his gang? So, here goes your story.

See, Hackett was a crazy sumbitch. Shot and killed a convenience store clerk for thirty bucks forty years ago, spent most of his life here in the joint. Anyway, he was always a little unpredictable, a little moody ... a lot like my wife.

Did I tell you about my wife already? Sherry once said, "Think of me, Charles, when you're in the bottom of a dumpster eating rat puke and J.D." Sherry and I were married for about twelve days. Thirteen if you count the day I found her in my king-sized waterbed with Michael the Plumber. No, not a real plumber. He was "The Plumber" for the same reason I'm "The Foot." It's how we take people out. He gets them with a copper pipe, sometimes a wrench, sometimes even a plunger. Sucked a guy's eyeballs out with one, I heard. When he was in a good mood, he shoved a funnel down someone's throat and opened up a bottle of Drano. The nicknames are a courtesy deal for us cold-blooders. Lets us all know who whacked who, so scores are straight and there's no confusion.

Well, I gave Sherry a couple good knocks, then I kicked The Plumber straight to hell. I kicked that fuck for so long I forgot who I was kicking by the time I was done, and with the bloody pulp on the floor choking on his own juice, and the warm water gushing outta the waterbed mattress—well, let's just say The Plumber couldn't remember his own nickname, either.

But that's not why I'm locked up in here. In fact, the pigs probably appreciated somebody taking The Plumber out of the game. The deal I cut saved my ass; no chair for me. Instead, I got a nice, comfy life on the inside in exchange for the names of certain cohorts and the blueprints for certain organizational structures. I'd be long gone if it weren't for that deal. *Cop killa*, as they say in here. 'Course, I didn't do that, 'cause it's a poor, dumb schlub who whacks a man with a shield. I was framed for that shit, see. And let me ... aw, crap, I've gone and digressed again.

So, anyways, Hackett got thrown into solitary for a couple days for losing his temper with a guard. He couldn't stand the place, he told me later. He grew up with ten brothers and four sisters, and then he got thrown in the joint, so he was used to being around a lot of people. The last time he got thrown in solitary he just about went shit-crazy, so we were all expecting him to come out white and wild-eyed. But, no. Sumbitch came out glowing ... fucking grinning! I asked him if he got some nice, imaginary ass in there, but he wouldn't talk about it. Wouldn't say a word. And then the next day he started a fight with Gunther the Idiot out in the yard.

Why's he "The Idiot?" Landmine gave him a good knock on the brain. Yeah, in fucking 'Nam. Where else, one of those pissy little Gulf wars? Gunther might not be The Idiot if he was in the Gulf. They got a little more respect for soldiers these days, but back then, you came back, couldn't get anybody to give two shits about your missing arm or leg, and next thing you knew, you were out on the fucking streets. You try coming back from an unpopular war after living in a bamboo cage, half-submerged in a river for two months with half your foot blown off, and trying to make a life. You wanna hear about my welcome home? How about living in Denver, stretching out my old man's sleeping bag beneath the interstate overpasses or digging out a crib in the bushes in City Park? With the zoo nearby, it was just like living in the jungle again.

The nicest place I stayed was in a scrapped semi trailer between the rail yards and a factory that looked abandoned except for the smokestack burning like a giant butt. On nice nights, I'd lay on my back on top of the trailer, light up a smoke I bummed off some asshole, stare up at the smokestack, and imagine it was my cigarette flaring up for all the world to see. People driving around at night would look out over the city lights and see that fire dancing in the darkness. My own fucking memorial.

That was right about the time I met Joey Perez. Met him in an all-night trucker joint. Gruff's Place. The punk at the door told me to get lost because I stank, and Joey Perez came up and knocked the fucker out, saying how he shouldn't be disrespecting the men who fought for our freedom. Guess Joey Perez had seen the Army tattoo on my arm. He won my respect right then and there.

Anyhow, it was Joey Perez who tried to get me to drop the habit. Smokes, I mean. He told me it wasn't cool no more. The attorney general said the shit was no good. I read about that crap, but coming from Joey's lips made it sound a little more truthful. Joey was always up with the times. He read the paper every morning, regardless of his current locale, inside the joint or out. He could be staying on a bench downtown and he'd panhandle and use the change to buy a newspaper and a cup of joe.

"The world is a backstabber, Chuck. You gotta know what's goin' on everywhere because you never know who's in the alley with you." He did most of his jobs in alleys. The throats of the world, he called them. A fucking poet.

"See, a town is like a man," he used to tell me. "Its head is the government and corporations and country clubs ('course, its head is usually up its ass), its body is the average schlub makin' a few bucks but not livin' it up, and its feet are the workin' men, who do all the real shit. And then there are the bowels, somewhere between the average schlub and the workin' man."

I've found that the bowels of a city are the best places to hang and lay low—whore motels, all-night tattoo parlors—but sometimes you gotta move higher up on the body to stay alive and sane. A city's got its bright sides and its dark sides, and Joey Perez taught me you gotta live in a town like you'd live with a woman. Get to know it until you realize it ain't safe to be sticking around any more, and right when you can't stand it, you move on to the next one. That's what Joey Perez always said.

**

Where was I? Yeah. So, Hackett tackled The Idiot like they were playing football. Gunther didn't do nothing, either ... well, other than his usual smack talk. He wasn't even talking to Hackett, but he got wailed on, anyway. Helluva fighter, Hackett. I'm glad I never faced him one-on-one. Then, when Hackett went back into solitary, we thought for sure that sumbitch was gonna come out dumber than The Idiot. But that sucker was happier than the first time he came out. So he gave the same damn beat down a week later, only this time to Farley, which wasn't such a good move, since Farley ruled things around here.

Not that I cared. The Foot don't kneel for no one. Not long after I landed in here, Farley and his gang tried to rough me up in the showers, and that was when I decided that I needed to let the locals know exactly how I got my nickname. Back in the day, Joey Perez had hooked me up with a sculptor friend of his, who cast a nice set of bronze toes for me. Y'know, so I could balance a little easier after 'Nam. Sure, it hurts a little when I give people the foot, but pain's a part of the life.

After the shower incident, I used a couple stones from the yard to sharpen up my bronze toes. And ever since I put holes in Benny's kidney, Farley's gang has pretty much steered clear of my soapy ass.

Hackett wasn't so lucky. I knew Farley would fuck him up, and I wanted to know why he was so hell-bent to get himself thrown in solitary. So I struck up a friendly little conversation with ol' Hackett at suppertime one night.

"What the fuck you come out so happy for, Hackett?"

"I don't know what you're talking about," he said.

"Like hell you don't. You got yourself thrown into solitary on purpose. I saw it. What the hell's in there that's so goddamned special?"

He looked at me, offended. "Don't take the name of the Lord in vain," he said.

So I grabbed him by the collar of his prison denim, and I said, "Fuck the Lord. What's goin' on in solitary?"

He stared at me, scared—and The Foot knows fear when he sees it. I think maybe I was the only one in here that he was afraid of. Funny, for a guy who was a helluva fighter. Anyhow, I let him sit back down. He looked around the cafeteria, and I followed his eyes. I noticed Farley and his cronies glancing over at some old man. That's one dead old man, I was thinking.

"It's a necklace."

"What the fuck are you talkin' about, a necklace?"

He slammed his fist down on the table and our paper dishes bounced. His milk spilled down the table, but he didn't seem to notice. His eyes were crazy-wild. Maybe solitary did push him over. But then I saw that it was a pleasure-crazy ecstasy. Lust, but not for anything normal like a woman.

"Grandma used to tell me a story. One of those wish-tales. You know what I'm talking about?"

"Like the wishbone?"

"Yes! Like the wishbone! Yes." He stroked his chin and his eyes jerked around like he hadn't slept in days. "She said there was once an evil wizard who imprisoned a princess in a tower. A huge tower on the top of a mountain. An enchanted tower. If she left the tower, she would die. Drop dead with her first step outside. And if anyone came to visit or rescue her, they would fall down dead, and she would have to live with the knowledge that she was responsible for their deaths."

"So, you got it on with a princess in solitary confinement?"

"The wizard cursed her. She would live there for the rest of her days. But he gave her one gift, a chain necklace with this little jewel on it. Like an amulet. While she wore it, whenever the clasp worked its way down to touch the amulet, she would know that someone she knew was thinking about her. She would make a wish for that person, and then she would pull the clasp back up behind her neck."

"Why didn't she just pull it down to touch the amulet so she could make a shitload of wishes?"

"It wouldn't work. It only functioned when someone thought of her. She could feel the clasp move down toward the amulet, and she could count the hours and minutes until another thought of her occurred to someone she knew."

"What the fuck are you talkin' about?"

"I'm saying I found that necklace! I survived solitary by living in the thoughts and memories of my family and friends. I'm escaped!"

He really had been pushed over.

"That's a bunch of crap, Hackett."

"It's real," he said. The guy's eyes ... like he was strung out, but ten times worse. "It's real."

"Why don't you just bring it out here, man? You're gonna get yourself killed if you keep pickin' fights."

But he was looking around the cafeteria like a hawk searching for mice, looking for another ticket to solitary, and I was getting a little nervous with Farley and his gang glancing over at us, so I took my cornbread and meatloaf over to another table. After all, Joey Perez always said, "You never know who's in the alley with you." And I wasn't about to walk down any alley with Hackett at my side. Farley was in the shadows.

The next morning, I was glad I had a smart buddy like Joey Perez. I woke up, and Hackett was stone cold, busted up and bleeding out of every hole in his body. I guess he pissed off Farley one too may times, and what could he expect but a long, black sleep after that?

Hackett's fairy story kept keeping me up nights. Maybe I liked that princess-in-the-tower shit. I wasn't sure why she'd leave her precious necklace in this shit hole, but it was worth checking out. And if it wasn't there, then at least I'd start sleeping again. Loose ends don't suit The Foot.

So, one day, I wailed on some fresh fish just come in for first degree. The kid ran over his parents on their front lawn with his buddy's H2 because Ma and Pa didn't want him going out that night. Dumb kids doing dumb shit.

I got solitary for beating up the punk, and I didn't find shit. When I got out, I still wasn't sleeping. I figured the necklace must be in a different cell, so I punched a guard in the jaw, got a little more backlash than I expected, because the guards weren't keen on saving my ass too quickly this time around. I won me a free trip to the infirmary for a cracked rib and broken nose. Then solitary.

And I found it. I fucking found it! A fucking necklace under a loose panel in the floor. The old man wasn't completely insane. It was an ugly thing, a scratched-up plastic amulet shaped like a little doll with all the paint rubbed off, missing one leg, a leather cord right through a hole in its head. So, I put it on, but it barely fit over my head. I have a big, egg-shaped head, y'know, but you can't see it when my hair's long, which is how I kept it before I got in here. I pulled the knot up to the back of my neck, and I sat and waited. Hours went by. Not a goddamned thing.

I was about ready to pull it off when I looked down and saw the knot right next to the little doll's head. And then the dark cell disappeared. I wasn't in solitary anymore. There was a woman in blue, a nurse, a bright room, big hospital beds, and an old woman lying in one of them. I was in the other bed, and I looked down at my hands where I was holding a photograph of myself wearing my private's uniform, just about to ship out to 'Nam. The hands holding the photograph were old and wrinkled. Then it was all gone and I was back in the cell.

So, I pulled the knot back up to my neck, waited for it to move down from my head to the doll's head again, and when it did, I was in a big, fat body talking to a lady in a dark bar. I was talking about The Foot, the quiet man who was always a kick at parties. The lady was laughing.

"The Foot was a great guy," the fat guy said. "Wish you could meet him, but he's in the joint now." And then I was back in the cell again, trying to figure out just who I was looking at just then. It was getting me higher than any dust ever had, so I kept looping that knot back up to my neck, and by the time they dragged me out of solitary, I was as giddy as a teenager after his first fuck.

After a while, I found out that I could make people do things––the people thinking about me. Only sometimes, though. Only when the people were mad or they were cursing my name.

That's how I found Sherry again. She was in a shit hole of an apartment, had a baby crying somewhere, maybe hers, with cigarette butts smoking themselves in ashtrays and dishes all over the place. I felt something pushing into us, and when I looked down I saw an ugly-ass man lying on the bed beneath me, his mouth moaning and his eyes straining in pre-orgasm like they were trying to keep him from dying. I looked down to see Sherry's naked body stretching down before my eyes, and that fat old man squeezing her tits—and it fucking hurt!—and clumsily thrusting inside us like he ain't gotten any in forty years.

Sherry was remembering the good screwing we got done in our twelve days of marriage and all the times beforehand, and she was trying to block out the face of this sumbitch. If only she'd known I was right there with her, feeling sorry that she had to whore herself out and hoping the same as she did that the fat fuck paid the fifty bucks he owed her for this one, plus the fifty from last week. Then it was all gone again.

I got tossed in solitary three times in the month I found that necklace. Like I said, The Foot don't like loose ends. So, I got thinking that I should start taking care of some unfinished business in the outside world.

And that's how I rubbed out Opie and half his gang. None of those guys had very fond memories of me, and every time my memory came up it was like a fucking civil war in Opie's territory.

I popped into Bumper's head right in the middle of a bank job—
—he and I did a bank in Carson City once and I yelled at him because
he was being a dumb ass by trying to rip off this chick's skirt. So I
was there in his head, and I swung around his sawed-off 12 and blew
Chopper across the lobby. Then I saw Rennie fire at me, and it hurt
like shit and the world was flying around me ... and then I was back
in the cell again. And I chuckled because they were all wearing *Star
Wars* masks for disguises, but I still knew who they were because
Bumper knew who they were.

I busted up a few more of Opie's men, making sure it was the
work of The Foot—kicking their brains out. Eventually, Opie thought
of me. Wondered how I could be out after he paid off Joey Perez to
frame me for nailing some star cop in Houston. The cop had a family of five, medals of honor, community service cred. Might as well
have been Christ hisself. Joey Perez did the kicking on that pig,
made it look like the handiwork of The Foot, which came off legit
because of how well he knew me. And because I didn't read the
paper enough. See, I didn't know who was in the alley with me.

So, I took Opie on a search for Joey Perez. Even though Joey
never let anybody know his whereabouts, I knew exactly where he
was. Joey Perez had made the mistake of walking down the alley
with me, but he didn't know I'd be back in the throat of the world
again.

It was an easy hunt since Opie wouldn't stop thinking of me. He
was worried The Foot was after him, and his mind was racing with
terror at the thought of The Foot sneaking up in the dark. I laughed,
and it came out as Opie's weasely little laugh. He was stripping
down a mickied little boy for a little stress-relief when I popped into
his head. Kid couldn't have been more than ten. I walked outta the
room, told one of Opie's men to get the kid dressed and to drop him

off at the school where he found him. Then I headed out the door and onto a first-class to Austin.

We found Joey Perez in his favorite hotel bed with Sherry, completely strung-out, bruises up and down her chunky arms. It surprised me to find her there, but then again, every chick I ever introduced to dreamy Joey Perez grew a soft spot for his slick talk. I wanted the Judas-lovin' bastard to know who was whacking him, so I shook him awake and said, "Hey, Joey Perez. It's me, Chuck." He looked at me like I was crazy, but he also looked a little resigned too. Like he always knew he'd get whacked someday.

But he still didn't believe it was me, so I delivered a series of kicks with Opie's steel-tipped boots that broke every bone in Joey Perez's body. I looked in his eyes to make sure he was afraid, but I left him alive because I knew he was gonna hurt for the rest of his fucking life. I crushed his throat to keep him from talking. That was more outta old habit than anything. What could he say against The Foot, anyway?

Next, I scooped up Sherry, who didn't wake up through the whole thing, and I flung our bodies through the window of room 517, Joey's favorite room in Austin. See, he'd made the mistake of falling in love with a city. And even though he was always leaving to do jobs here and there, he always returned to that town. But it betrayed him, piece of trash city that it was. Even in the middle of the night, it was eighty degrees out there and humid as hell. Opie was sweating like a fucking pig as we plunged to the ground. I knew he was in there somewhere, watching all this from the back of his own brain, not able to do a fucking thing.

That jump was my special touch. I had heard God don't look kindly on His folks committing suicide, and all Opie ever talked about was being Catholic and Christ-this and Christ-that. Course, I thought, as the hood of a Buick came flying up, Sherry's hair tossing around in my face, I doubt He looks too kindly on organized crime or pedophilia, either.

Why'd I take Sherry with me? You think she was making a good life in the world? I took her because I fucking loved her. I saved her.

So, that's how I took care of some loose ends on the outside. These days I'm toying with Farley and his boys, getting them to fight each other. Soon I think I'll have Farley drop his soap. That'll shake up his little gang a bit.

Why don't I just break outta here? You know what kind of a mess that'd be? I'd need a little more help than some telepathic control. I can't control everybody at once. Besides, I kinda like it in here, in my own little tower. I feel pretty damn safe these days, and I'm getting used to being a little more sociable. These days, it pays to make an impression.

I broke the rules a little. I couldn't get myself thrown into solitary forever; they look down on that shit. So, I decided I'd bring the necklace out here in the open, and it still works just fine. If only Hackett had known. Lots of power in this little woman. And I've come to notice when the knot touches the right side of her head, people are remembering me nicely; y'know, like flowers and songs and shit. Like my mother did that first time I put it on. Stuck in some nursing home, mind gone, but she sometimes remembers she had a son who never came back from a long-ago war, thinking, "I hope he's happy wherever he is now." Sometimes someone I don't know, someone I don't remember, remembers me on the right side of the doll's head. Playin' in a sandbox with other kids—"He's always digging holes, that guy." Throwing stones at the alley cats—"He's a good shot, that kid." Cashing a fat government check at a grocery store—"He's not bad looking, if only he'd shave." And then thoughts in a foreign language, Vietnamese, looking down at a cage half-submerged in a river, at the haggard, wild-eyed skeletons of men standing inside, a strange crimson pulsing, a pain in the eyes like confusion and regret and undeserving—"How could I have tortured those people?" And then they're gone.

But the knot usually falls to the left side of this little doll's head. And that's when I can take charge of things. And it's happening more now that rumors of The Foot escaping prison are circulating through the underworld, or that someone's doing revenge work for The Foot. The thoughts and memories are plenty. Come to think of it, if I worked hard, I bet I could break outta here. I have a feeling the wizard's story was bullshit. The princess could have left that tower anytime and anybody could have come in to see her. I bet she liked her power, and I bet she killed anybody who came to rescue her.

The way I see it, I can live out there in the alley, watching the shadows and always looking over my shoulder. Or I can *be* the alley, and I don't have to walk down it with nobody. I'm the shadows, and I'm the throat of the fuckin' world, see.

Teachers' Pets

BY MICHAEL CIPRA

On my first day of teaching, I was quite nervous. Having been raised and educated in a rural setting, studying geometry and grammar in a disintegrating farmhouse and developing my earliest sensibilities among cows and pigs, I was worried that the students at your school would be more sophisticated than I.

Upon reflection, perhaps I overcompensated for my insecurities, pushing the children too hard, taking my job past all acceptable limits, following a logical series of steps beyond the point where such logic could possibly be beneficial. Mr. Falch, I will take the blame. No one can deny, however, that our situation was extreme.

As I was saying, on my first day I was quite nervous. However, the children bounded into their desks with such light hearts and spontaneous laughter that they immediately put me at ease. Upon being told to open their books, the children did not groan or become impersonal as I had expected; in fact, their faces were as rapt as before, the joy just as plain as they stared down at the formulas that explained the relationships between angles and triangles, slaves and masters, skyscrapers and architects. What brilliant pupils, I thought. What potential!

We got through the first chapter in World History—*The Reign of the Cave Men*—before the storm that destroyed most of downtown began in earnest. We were recreating the *Lascaux* cave paintings on a piece of butcher paper when a tremendous roar shook the foundation of the school. I ran to the windows, and threw them open. Outside, kites flew wildly, and pigeons hid in the alcoves of the school, cooing into the disturbed air. Above the school, great black clouds built, storm clouds like nothing I had seen, clouds like a fleet of aircraft carriers floating through the sky.

"A terrible storm is coming," I said. "You must all get home."

"But what about *Lascaux*?" they cried. "We want our lesson."

"Your homework is to finish drawing the horned creature of your choice goring the stick figure of a man," I said. "Tomorrow, we will move on to the Greeks. Now you must leave."

"We want to improve ourselves," said some.

"We want better jobs," said others.

"Our parents will beat us if we come home without learning," said a few.

The first huge drops of rain hit the windowsills. They sounded like hammers in a dark tunnel, and the children became even more reluctant to leave the sanctuary of the school.

"You will all survive," I said. "When you go outside, hold your books over your heads to keep dry."

I demonstrated with a dictionary, opening to the letter *L* and placing the book's pages over my head like a hat. The children laughed. When I took the dictionary off my head, the first word I saw was "lummox." The second was "lumbago," which, in case you didn't know, is a painful form of rheumatism, which affects the muscles and tendons of the lower back. My aunt has a particularly bad case. Later, of course, we burned this dictionary for warmth.

"Perhaps we can spend a minute or two more in class," I said cautiously. I didn't want the lesson to end while they were laughing at me.

The children cheered.

Mr. Falch, I didn't go into tremendous detail; I took only a few moments to explain how our pre-historic ancestors hunted, how they stayed alive through the cold of the last ice age, and how they sucked the hot marrow from animal bones. The whole time, I had a terrible feeling about the storm outside. I could barely hear my pupils breaking imaginary mammoth femurs because the rain was so loud.

"Class dismissed!" I finally cried. Together, we stuffed all of the children's things into their backpacks. Someone had brought a Chihuahua to class. I put the Chihuahua in a backpack, too. The children looked like overburdened Sherpas with all of that gear strapped to their small bodies. Although they didn't want to do it (they complained of looking silly), I made them put books on top of their heads. I was very adamant on that score. No one can accuse me of not considering the welfare of those children.

Mr. Falch, as you know, the alarm system was not working on the fourth floor. My class (the only class conducted at that elevation) was not given proper warning about the coming storm. True enough, I taught for a few extra minutes. But isn't that my job? By the time we got organized enough to descend three flights of stairs, the entire first floor had flooded and water was inching up the stairs. The children were philosophical.

"We don't want to die in your wretched school," they said.

"No one's going to die," I assured them. "And this school isn't so wretched."

"Will we have to eat each other?" asked the largest child, a mountainous, pigtailed girl named Ella Johnson.

"Let me be clear," I said. "No one's going to eat anyone else."

"I'm hungry," said a voice from the back of the group.

"I have to pee," said someone else.

"All right," I said. "Everyone back up to the fourth floor. We'll figure things out up there."

We marched, books atop our heads, back to the classroom where everything had begun ... back to the small, uncomfortable room where we would make our stand against nature.

Mr. Falch, you must have known that your school had a particularly large and presumptuous rat population. Huge, smelly, unafraid ... or perhaps you didn't know. I myself had no idea that rodents were attracted to this seat of learning until the second day of the flood.

We had just eaten the last of our carefully rationed food. No more warm bologna sandwiches. Morale was on the decline. As an attempt at inspiration, I decided to teach a lesson centered on American History. The children tittered as I told them how their forefathers had dumped caskets of tea into the harbor (I picked up Jimmy Chamberlain and carried him to the window as a visual aid). I don't mean to brag, but I delivered quite a rousing lecture. When I got to the part about shooting British soldiers in the back, there was a scurrying over our heads. I stopped in mid-sentence, just as a revolutionary was raising his musket from the cover of the trees. The scurrying continued.

Evidently still shaken from our reenactment of the tea party, Jimmy Chamberlain yelled out, "It's the Redcoats!"

I knew better, but I wasn't about to tell those innocent children what was probably sharing the fourth floor with us. I returned to Valley Forge.

On the third day, the Chihuahua disappeared. At the time, we didn't know what had happened to our little pet, but the loss of edible flesh was a serious psychological setback. Many suspected Ella Johnson (the big girl always gets blamed). I figured the dog just ran away, out of some canine sense of self-preservation. Our hunger pains were becoming quite obvious.

On the fourth day of captivity, Ella went searching for something to eat. She grumbled an apology for skipping out on my grammar lesson and lunged out of class. Ella's scream, no more than a minute later, was horrible and beautiful, moving through the air like a creature with wings. I abandoned prepositional phrases and ran down the hall. Just inside the door of the planned J.C. Falch Discovery Room, Ella stood motionless, her pigtails hanging like icicles. In the middle of the room lay the scoured bones of our Chihuahua.

At this point, the students began whispering to each other. All of them were aware of some force apart from the flood with which we had to contend, some strange, preternatural force. In the pauses between gastronomical maydays, the children heard scuttling feet. When they looked at the bookcase, they saw small yellow eyes peering from behind copies of *World Cultural Perspectives*. Several children cried in their sleep. Others held hands. I believe my students smelled rat urine, as I did, on the ceiling boards above us.

My own way of dealing with this unorthodox situation was to throw myself into lesson preparation. I designed activities, quizzes, lectures, role-playing situations ... anything that would facilitate learning in the subjects I had been hired to teach. The students tried their best, but I believe the combination of fear, hunger, and fatigue prevented them from absorbing much of value. All lessons are documented in the class folder. You see, Mr. Falch, even in our darkest hour, I fulfilled the terms of my contract. I taught until education was no longer a sane pursuit. I taught far beyond that point.

The stakes got higher for everyone on the fifth day. At dusk, Stan Parker walked unsteadily down the hall to the bathroom. He never came back.

The next morning, I took apart three of the school's desks (the cost of which I see you have deducted from my severance pay) and disseminated to my students the aluminum bars that had previously held the desks together. Yes, I am aware that distributing metal bars to the students is a Class II violation of the school weapons policy. Mr. Falch, I wish to reiterate: ours was an extreme situation.

To continue, I spent the morning of this sixth day on some introductory zoology. Incidentally, the Schutts and Miller text that you provide for the children has an excellent series of diagrams related to the rodent family. Ah, you already know.

In the afternoon, I sent the students out in groups of three and four. In my estimation, I had long neglected the children's physical education; starvation was an appropriate excuse, but still, a bit of exercise couldn't hurt. Or could it?

Unfortunately, we lost one group. Cathy Meek, Steven Willoughby, and little Jimmy Chamberlain never returned from physical education. The rest of us, however, came back with some two-dozen dead rats, bludgeoned, skewered, kicked, and (in the case of several rodents that encountered Ella Johnson) stepped on. Our mood was cautiously festive. I set four or five books on fire, and we gave the rats a perfunctory roasting before devouring them. Although rat flesh is not the best thing for the digestive tract of a starving child or even a starving adult (several of us retched), you must admit that we had few other options. After all, one cannot eat books.

The attendance chart reveals that when class began on the seventh day, only three of the original twelve students were present: Ella Johnson, Mike Middlemarch, and Sweet Pea Monroe. This is not a careless mistake. I called roll five times. The rest of my students, I have to assume, were not sick, nor were they playing hooky. In your current attendance system, however, there is no way to notate "snatched by rats in the middle of the night." (Without much effort, the attendance system could be revamped to deal with such contingencies.)

In any case, you have noticed that on the seventh day overall attendance actually took a dramatic leap in spite of the loss of several of the original pupils.

The remaining students were understandably opposed to the idea of welcoming rats into the student body. Mike Middlemarch, with fresh bruises and bite marks all over his face, couldn't stop crying. Sweet Pea Monroe had nothing but contempt to offer her new classmates; she had a tendency to lash out rather frequently with the metal bar I had given her (Yes, Mr. Falch, all discipline problems are noted in the progress reports). Ella, of course, just wanted to eat them.

The rats themselves insisted that they were good rats, friendly and kind, and that a rival faction was responsible for decimating our numbers. Having interspecies allies seemed like an excellent idea at the time. I questioned the rats as to their dedication, for I had never known rats to be creatures to seek a formal education. What were their goals? What did they stand to gain from my tutelage?

"We want a better life," said some.

"We want to get rich," said others.

"Fine food."

"Pretty rat wives."

In short, the rats recognized that the flood would soon near its end, and the prospect of an uncertain future terrified them. Mr.

Falch, surely you know that education has historically been a way out of darkness and uncertainty for the lower classes, a way of stepping to the next social and economic level. Why couldn't education be an *evolutionary* stepping-stone as well? Coming from a poor rural background, I sympathize with all creatures judged too coarse for respectable society. Perhaps that's why I reached out to the rats; maybe that's why I put my knowledge at the disposal of vermin.

My first and only day of mixed-species teaching was a complete disaster. All of the original pupils were lost. Sweet Pea was the first to go, disappearing down the hall during nutrition break. Mike jumped from the window in the midst of an economics lesson; apparently the laws of supply and demand were too much for his troubled mind to confront.

Ella snacked on one of her classmates for most of the morning, but when it was time for anatomy, the rats had their revenge. I tried to divert them with diagrams of the human body, but it was no use. The rats piled on Ella until I could no longer see her flesh; there was simply a mountain of rodents, running, jumping, scurrying over the prone form of my last human student. I threatened to expel the rats. No one listened.

What's that, Mr. Falch? Are you suggesting that there were no rats at all, that it was only us the whole time, just a room full of cannibals and murderers? A haunting statement, sir. But believe me or don't believe me: there were rats.

So why am I still alive? I'll tell you; the rats—and there were about two hundred at this point—were hungrier for an education than they were for me. I could keep breathing as long as I kept teaching. You can well imagine the pressure this puts on an educator, particularly one who has lost faith in the social fabric that ties teacher to students. Yes, the structure of education can exist even when the spirit has been removed.

Over the course of the next three days, I taught nonstop. My lessons were a blur of algebra and geometry, a whirlwind of rhetoric, a collage of biology, world history, and foreign language. In essence, my students had to digest all of western culture in three days ... in addition to digesting the rest of Ella Johnson.

I found myself skipping over literature, as the vermin found it boring. Mythology was also largely irrelevant to the rats, although they liked the general concept of Prometheus getting his liver pecked to bits. In economics, however, my new pupils excelled, drawing logical conclusions from complicated masses of fact and number. Politics also inspired a remarkable acuity in the rats. In fact, their natural ability in these areas frightened me. I looked into yellow eyes and saw a mercenary intelligence, a cold grasp of what it meant to have. Or not to have.

Biology sparked a legitimate interest in them, as well, but my authority as a science teacher was seriously undermined when I told the rats their place on the evolutionary ladder. A wave of violent dissent filled the class; books were eaten in protest. A few particularly rebellious students bit my ankles. Things didn't settle down until I completely recanted, modifying the chart that I had placed on the board, so that the letters R-A-T sat atop the pyramid of oceanic and terrestrial life.

On the third day of teaching rats (my tenth day overall), the flood waters dropped dramatically. I could hear helicopters whirling around the city. We all knew the end was near. As I looked out into row after row of shining teeth, as I searched pair after pair of glittering eyes for a sign, I wondered if I had taught any of my pupils what it meant to be decent creatures. Mr. Falch, how do you teach mercy? Can compassion be conveyed in a classroom setting? By this time, I had oozing wounds all over my body. The rats laughed and called them love-bites. I went to bed that eleventh night not expecting to live through my nightmares.

Around three in the morning, I awoke in excruciating pain. My students were crowded around my left leg, feeding on me. I grabbed the nearest object, which providentially happened to be a compass from the afternoon's geometry lesson. I plunged my compass into the nearest rat. The pointed end went through his belly, and he squealed. I extracted the compass and stabbed another rat through the eye. The rodents momentarily scattered.

I stood, hoping that the damage to my leg was not crippling. Survival demanded that I get to the window quickly and jump from it into the swirling waters below. The rats were startled by my aggression and mobility. They must have thought that I was just a weak and ineffectual educator. Ha! Take that! I hobbled to the window, skewering two more along the way. At the windowsill, I barely had time to unlatch the portal and push it open before they were all over me, clinging to my clothes, hanging from my skin. Their blood was mixing with mine, and suddenly, I had a delirious wave of clarity.

How could I communicate with rats? Why was I the only person left? What if, in all of my vicious struggles to survive, I had become the thing I despised, the thing that was now trying to consume me?

Mr. Falch, don't laugh. I have lived low for so many days and nights in your school that anything is possible. I have prostituted education in room 404, not thinking of the consequences and the responsibilities of knowledge. One lesson led to the next by a chain of logic I never thought to question until I saw my students gnawing on my legs ... *according to my own instructions*! What subject can be taught with the certainty that it will be used in good faith? No such subject exists, unless every lesson is filled with the heart of the instructor.

When I jumped from the window, I didn't expect to survive. I was just hoping to take a few of the rats with me. The current took my pupils in a different direction, and I found myself atop a piece of driftwood. Two miles downstream, just past the stadium, I was rescued. I do not know where the rats went.

A rat with an education is a dangerous creature, Mr. Falch. You assure me that exterminators have been sent into your school and that the rat problem is being handled, even as we complete our final interview.

But that look on your face does not convince me.

Your sneer exposes a line of teeth, their stark edges high-lighted by the fluorescent glow in this room. Your eyes have a strange glitter tonight, Mr. Falch, and I am quite sure that I don't trust it. Before you take another step toward me, you should know that the compass I originally used to escape from your school is still in my pocket.

More importantly, I am prepared to use it.

The Price of a Bullet

BY CHANCE CLARK

I needed a fucking cigarette. And I aimed to get plenty of them when I cracked open that ancient cigarette machine back at the motel like some psychotic fiend. That was, if I didn't bleed to death first. My lower abdomen was still draining whiskey-scented blood at a fair pace, and I didn't expect it to stop any time soon, or at all for that matter.

Here's a little side note, kids: vitamin K helps the blood clot. Alcoholism, while tasty and fun, depletes vitamin K and ultimately increases the chance of death by paper cut. Now, you won't read this on the warning label of your next bottle of Jim Beam. The only reason I have a clue is because I slept with a pre-med student for a few weeks before my drinking finally turned her off. So trust me when I tell you, JB and his bottled buddies all have the potential of bleeding you out like a stuck pig. Then again, maybe I'm not the type of guy to be taking advice from.

Anyway.

The desert night was as cold and silent as Elvis. I was tired and weak and freezing and bleeding and pissed off as I buried the bodies at Devil's Cobblestone. That was the name given to the eerie cut of desert back when Las Vegas was just the Flamingo. And it lived up to its name.

Needless to say, the night had ended violently.

***

I hadn't had a smoke in nine days--my Lola's idea--and it was eating a jittery hole in my addiction, so I happily stepped into the thick haze of cigarette smoke and inhaled for a quick fix.

"I'll be at the bar, doll," I said.

"Okay, baby," Lola said with her velvety voice before gently biting my lip. "I'll just have to love you later, then."

I licked her flavor from my lips and watched as she sashayed away in a little black number she filled sensationally. Soon she disappeared into the drifting cloud of tuxedos and slinky dresses swaying throughout the ballroom of the Lampley Estate. It was yet another syndicate mixer–soirées where the egotistical assemble to admire each other, organized and executed the third Friday of each month.

These parties, I fucking hated them. Not so much the gatherings themselves, but most of the other lowlifes who were smug enough to attend them.

The festive clambakes were synonymous with the loose and fast of the Las Vegas crime syndicate, an organization controlled indirectly by the Lampley Brothers with a masturbatory stranglehold. I say indirectly because there was a handful of crusted old mugs out in the hills of Hollywood with much bigger dicks to swing. The brothers would have to answer to them if shit were to ever go haywire.

The smoky goodness called my name, and I sucked in another

healthy breath and headed toward the bar in a gleam of zombie boredom. As I passed through the meaningless chatter among guests, I noticed a murderous shade of red zigzagging through the gloom of the crowd. I tried to keep it in focus, but it faded away in a blur of nicotine cravings and one hell of a boozy thirst.

I slid up to the bar real smooth-like and ordered Jameson over rocks in a deep glass. When the dapper barkeep finally slapped it down onto the well-worn mahogany, I immediately swiped it up like some fiendish Viking pillaging village virgins. I took a solid swig and let the heavenly burn swirl deep in my chest like freshly siphoned gasoline.

With a secondhand cigarette buzz under my cumber bun and a ramped taste for alcohol in my system, I was ready to head home and strap Lola's ass on like a feedbag.

As that lovely thought wiggled in my pants, Terry Lampley saddled up next to me with what looked a hell of a lot like a Shirley Temple clutched in his sweaty little mitt. It matched the girlish smile spread all over his college-boy face.

"Johnny Boy, you have to meet my date, man," he said excitedly.

"Why, she hot?"

"Like an arsonist's wet dream."

"Well, that I gotta see."

"You'll have to give her a tick though, she's off taking a pee," he said, then sipped his pretty pink drink.

Terry was the youngest of the three Lampley Brothers and probably the closest thing to a best friend I'd had in ten years. I'd only known him for four.

"You seen Mitch yet?" he asked.

"No. Why?"

"I hear he's pretty pissed about this job you refused to do."

"What do you know about it?"

"Same as usual. Less than nothing."

Terry had little knowledge of the intricacies of the family business—partly by choice, partly by the choices of his brothers. And it was no secret that Terry held a mighty contempt for those two sons-of-bitches. Hell, that was probably why I liked him so damn much.

"The job was wrong," I said, and gestured for another Jameson, rocks.

"They're all wrong, Johnny," he said, shaking his head. "But are those really the decisions you want to be making off the cuff? Especially from behind closed doors with my brothers?"

He had a point—moot, but sharp. I was no schlub but I knew there were whispers of consequence. There always were. But sometimes a worthless mutt like me had to make choices for himself. I figured part of my job for the Lampleys was to administer advice. On paper, the Lampleys were investors of numerous hotels and casinos in the area, and I was no mathematician. But I was antisocial and borderline psychotic. And their real moneymakers were escort services, strip joints, low-end porno production companies, drugs, political corruption, and contract murder.

That was my niche—the murders. And who better to take advice from on the subject of killing than the cool killer himself? Like I said, the job was wrong.

"I'll smooth things over after this jamboree disperses," I said.

"That's in about an hour, bubba," Terry said.

"What are you talking about?"

"It's the twenty-first, man."

I looked at my wrist as though I owned a watch, and imagined if I had it would have been one that displayed the date.

"I guarantee Mitch will find you by then," he added.

"I was gonna slip out early anyway," I mumbled as I slurped

my cocktail.

Everyone would be cleared out of the mansion by midnight, even if it took gunfire to do it. Because twelve-thirty on the twenty-first of each month was reserved for the Banker.

The Banker was a mousy little crud who was the brains behind the hotel/casino illusion. The Lampleys paid him handsomely for false paperwork he brought by every month for their John Hancocks, and they sure as hell didn't want anyone around when they put pen to paper, or to risk the chance of anyone identifying their precious little Mousketeer on the inside.

Terry yammered something along the lines of "Blah, blah, blah." I shook my head as I drained my glass and ordered another Jameson, neat this time, just for kicks.

A dame's voice came from the other end of the bar, calling for Terry. It was one of the usual caterers. She was decent, and not so ugly that she was unattractive, but not so attractive that she wasn't ugly. I had no idea what her name was and didn't much care. I was more interested in the Marlboro she lit up.

"Mister Lampley," she said. "Do you have a spare corkscrew?"

"What's wrong with the one behind the bar?"

"It's missing and we need to open a few more bottles of red for the guests," she said with beautiful wisps of smoke floating from her mouth.

"Excuse me, doll," I cut in. "What's your name?"

She looked at me as though I had just appeared from a fog. "Eve."

"Well, Eve, sweetie, would you please be so generous as to smoke that thing this way?"

Eve smiled and took a hard drag. I watched the tip of the cigarette glow red and had a sudden desire to chew the tobacco-filled stick like a licorice whip. Eve brought her face close to mine with a hint of seduction, and gently exhaled. For a brief moment, I might have loved her, despite her half-ugliness.

"There should be a set of corkscrews in the kitchen, Eve," Terry said.

"Okay," she said, with me still caught in her gaze.

"I'll get one for you, doll," I told her. "Call it payback for the smoke."

Eve smiled and gave a slight Hitler-styled spin on her toes, then pranced away with a little extra sway in her hips. For my benefit, I assumed.

A thick mitt grabbed my shoulder. I turned around and Duke—one half of Mitch's two-man security detail—stood there with a sour look dripping from his puss.

"Hey, Johnny," he said.

"What's going on, Big Duke?"

"Mister Lampley would like to see you in his office."

"Thank you," I said, and turned back to my drink.

Duke squeezed my shoulder. "Now."

***

The quickest route to the upstairs office was through the foyer. I took the stairs at the back of the kitchen, laughing all the way to the polished oak doors of Mitch Lampley's lair, as though the extra twenty seconds were really sticking it to him.

I knocked and poked my head between the doors.

"Come on in, Johnny Boy," Mitch said huskily.

"You wanted to see me, Boss?" I asked as he stepped around his desk and embraced me like we were the Corleones.

"Yeah, have a seat."

I sat in one of the chairs positioned in front of the desk.

Carson Lampley sat in the other, silent, with a little smirk stemming from one corner of his mouth. Carson was the pretty one. Always well groomed and stinking of expensive cologne. He carried himself with a *GQ*, James Bond kind of swagger, and his mere presence in the room made me want to kill him and spit and piss on his corpse.

Mitch and Carson were the Frick and Frack of the Vegas underworld. Not that they were stupid or anything. In fact, they were quite cunning. But they lacked commonsense when it came to the big picture. That made them dangerous as well as reckless. Like ordering the murder of unimportant players, bringing heat and questions from the authorities they didn't have in their pockets.

Mitch returned to his desk without offering me a drink. He sat down and shook his bulbous head. His head reminded me of the swollen body of a blood-filled tick. He placed a sealed envelope in front of him with an exaggerated sigh. "What are we gonna do about this, Johnny Boy?"

My assignments came in the form of names, sealed in an unmarked envelope. If I left the office with the envelope and your name was in it, you had a day or two at best before I caught up with you. This envelope was different. I knew it contained the name I had already refused to cross out.

"I told you, I don't think it's the right decision," I said.

Mitch was silent. I could tell he was conflicted and probably felt I was losing my edge. And he was probably right. Maybe I didn't have it in me anymore.

"So what are you suggesting we do to rid ourselves of this little problem?" he said at last.

"If you're so serious about going through with it, pull someone in from Utah."

Carson scoffed. "It's not his choice to make, Mitch." Then he turned and looked me dead in the eyes. "He's just the help."

I wanted to shut him up by ripping his jaws apart with my bare hands and wearing the mandible bone as a decorative trophy around my neck like a savage cannibal. Instead, I opened my yap and with all the sincerity of a perturbed adolescent, I said, "You're not the boss of me."

There was an awkward moment of silence then Carson laughed like a hyena giving birth. "What a fucking idiot," he laughed.

That was when I realized I had spoken before my brain actually had the chance to proofread my thoughts.

Mitch calmed Carson down with a slight wave of his hand. "Carson's right, Johnny. It helps no one if every time I spit out a name you up and decide to add it to your Do Not Kill list, now does it? That's just not good business, Johnny, and I think you know that. Besides, I'd kind of like to keep this in-house, if you know what I mean."

I took a moment and seethed. "For four years I've accepted each and every envelope you've slid across this desk without question."

"That you have."

"That's a lot of envelopes," I said.

"Seventeen," Carson kicked in again.

"Yeah, a lot of envelopes," Mitch said, tapping the envelope in question with his finger. "So why not this one?"

I thought I might sound like a chump again, so I didn't answer.

"How 'bout a little something extra?" he said, setting a stack of cash on the envelope. "Something to get that shambles of a motel of yours up and running."

I looked long and hard at the cash, but couldn't see past the envelope at the bottom.

"We would like to have this taken care of by week's end," Carson said patronizingly.

"Pull someone in from Utah," I said.

Mitch sighed. Carson scoffed.

I knew their reach into Utah was shoulder deep, because well over half the girls they employed were imported from the clutches of a strict Mormon upbringing. Fresh-faced girls with addictive personalities who begged to be loosened and freed from their childhoods.

Lola was one of those girls. She had come to the Lampleys at the age of nineteen and was passed around the organization like a common cold, being used and abused. She liked it that way. Carson was the last of the bastards to be with her, thus my hysterical hatred for the creep.

Mitch shook his head. "I'll let this go only once," he said with an evil seriousness. "But from now on, you do for me. A name to me is a bullet to you. Do you understand me?"

I understood that he was leading me on because there was no way in hell he was going to drop this thing without serious repercussions. But I thanked him anyway.

***

I wasn't too happy with the way the conversation with Mitch went, but all I could do was try to push it to the back of my head. Strangely enough, I caught a whiff of Lola's perfume as I descended the staircase leading back to the kitchen. It made me crazy. It made me want her on the spot—our bodies grinding together, scuffed and torn and bleeding on the wooden stairs.

Once in the kitchen, I rummaged through the drawers, searching for a corkscrew for the not-so-lovely Eve. Most of the snobbish utensils were sterling and had a queer little *L* monogrammed on them, engraved in some fancy calligraphic-style. I was shoving shit back and forth, making quite the clatter, when Terry came pushing through the swinging doors.

"Hey, do you have the corkscrew, asshole?" he asked.

"Nah, I'm pretty sure I have one of your run-of-the-mill, plain-jane assholes, but you'll have to give me a few minutes alone if you want confirmation."

"Not interested." He went to a group of cabinets and pulled out a box set of sterling corkscrews. "You don't have the tits for it."

"I gotta get out of here," I said, slamming the drawer.

"Went that well, huh?"

"I think we came to an understanding."

"Good," he said, sneaking a glance around him.

"What is it?"

"I've been thinking of getting out of here, myself," he whispered. "Getting out and disappearing."

I was talking about getting out of the house. Terry was talking about getting out of the life. Distancing himself from the Lampley name, from his brothers, from Las Vegas.

"Mitch has been stashing money away in a false floor in the back of his closet for years," he said. "I could take that money and vanish, and re-emerge with a new name for a chance at a new life in a new city ..."

It all sounded so bizarre falling from his lips, but the more he talked, the more it seemed like a plan he was prepared to put into motion.

"How much loot are we talkin' about?"

"Seven, maybe eight-hundred grand, easy."

"So, what's keeping you here?" I asked.

"My brothers."

***

Terry led us out of the kitchen and through a sea of wine drinkers where I subtly stepped on every foot I could before we reached the bar, and when we did, I ordered another Jameson.

I gave grim-faced Eve the corkscrew and she gave me her business card in return and told me to give her a call sometime. I smiled and stuffed the card into my pocket. I could always burn it later.

"Hey, Johnny," Terry said. "Here she comes."

I turned around and saw Terry's date parting the crowd like Moses himself, only she wasn't wearing rags. No, she was barely dressed at all, in a sexy, devil-red dress. I was sure Terry had picked out the wardrobe specifically for the occasion to better flaunt her villainous figure. No doubt she was the crimson comet I had noticed blazing through the ballroom. And Terry was right too— she was gorgeously designed for sex: sleek, muscular features, and firm, store-bought tits, all wrapped in caramel skin.

She had leaned in and kissed Terry with a little more than her full lips when I noticed the back of the dress. It swooped so low it revealed a small tattoo of the astrological sign of the planet Mars and an inviting, half inch of ass-crack.

Terry smiled. "Johnny Boy, this is Carnival. Carnival, baby, this is Johnny Boy."

"Hello, Johnny," she said with a sultry voice before kissing me on the cheek.

"Carnival," I said. "Such an attractive and intriguing name."

"Thank you so much. I chose it myself."

Most of the men around the bar were completely enthralled with Carnival's sexual charisma, and kept a lustful eye on her as the three of us talked, drank, and laughed. It amused me, because as closely as these perverts were gawking, I could almost guarantee none of them was perceptive enough to notice the small lump in her throat or the larger one in the crotch of her dress.

Terry didn't consider himself a homosexual, but half of a heterosexual. I mean, he loved women. He just loved them a little more with dangling male organs.

Time was creeping up on midnight and people were beginning to filter out of the mansion. I told Terry and Carnival to enjoy the rest of their night, and with the hungry smiles they shot back at me, I knew they would and then some. And I couldn't help but wonder if Terry had the balls to take Mitch for his hidden loot and somehow manage to fade away with Carnival to some exotic, far-off land. A piece of me hoped he did.

I needed a cigarette. I found myself staring into ashtrays filled with spent butts, wondering if anyone would notice if I popped one into my mouth and sucked it down like a Tic-Tac. I meandered through the thinning crowd until I spotted Lola saying her goodnights to Carson with a hug. My eyes caught hers and she quickly shied away from him, knowing how insane I could get.

"You ready to go, doll?" I asked.

"Yeah, baby," she answered, wrapping herself around my shoulders.

Carson smiled a sly type of smile that made me wonder if the feathers of a canary might float out if he were to open his mouth. He coolly reattached a Barbied-up dame to each arm and said, "Stay safe, Johnny Boy."

No feathers.

I said nothing, but wished him dead.

***

Outside, a flock of guests migrated toward their foreign-made automobiles and chauffeured limousines beneath the magnificent glow of a full moon.

The top was already reclined on my vintage Lincoln Continental, and I was looking forward to the cool, desert wind against my face. I jammed the key into the ignition and cranked it over until the engine roared, then purred.

Lola nestled herself into the leather upholstery and gazed over at me. "Go ahead, baby," she said softly.

Her eyes were a pale shade of smoldering blue, but in the sheen of moonlight they looked a luminous, coyote-grey. She moistened her lips with her tongue and gently pulled her dress up to the bend of her hips as she eased her head back against the seat in an ultimate display of vulnerability.

There was no more talk. I pasted her a good one high across the cheek and it came off with the cracking sound of paddled flesh. The force whipped her head to the side, and I couldn't determine whether what I heard from her was a whimper or a moan, but she whipped right back around and spit in my face. I grabbed a handful of her hair and pulled her mouth into mine, hard. Our mouths slipped together with tongues and spit as Lola gripped my zipper. She pulled back long enough to shoot me a beautifully pornographic grin. Then she eagerly put her mouth to work.

I barely noticed half of the Las Vegas underworld pattering by like mindless drones as I kicked the car into drive and eased it out of the overbearing iron gates.

The wind felt amazing.

***

I owned a seedy, secluded roadside motel that most honest people hoped like hell they would never have to spend a pee in, much less an entire night. It was a questionable investment: two rickety ice machines that froze a nice glaze of amber rust to the cubes, a dingy, rat infested office that even I refused to enter on account of a fear of rodents, one old-fashioned cigarette vending machine, which I kept stocked and hidden in number six for whenever I started smoking again, and twelve, lovely rooms decorated in antique dust and peeling paint, with the subtle fragrance of sauteed scrotum and Elmer's Glue.

I lived in number nine, and still had the faint notion that one day I'd actually flip on the 'vacancy' sign.

I pulled the Lincoln right up to number nine and shoved it into park as Lola pulled her wet mouth off of me with the sound of a popped cork. We wrestled our way out of the car and halfway out of our clothes before we stumbled into my room and crashed to the floor. Lola quickly started right back up where she left off, only this time she accented it with some of the filthiest talk I've ever heard coming from such a pretty dame's mouth. I twirled her around and sat her on my face, and decided the night was finally going my way. We ended up swapping so much fluid over that next hour and a half that we may have actually switched DNA.

Afterwards, I foolishly asked Lola if I could have a cigarette.

"Just because you lit me up like a Molotov Cocktail, baby, doesn't mean I'm gonna forget what you promised me, now does it?"

"No, I guess not."

"I will share a drink with you though, baby," she said then gently bit my nipple.

I managed to get some fluid circulating in my legs and I slipped out the door and down to number two where I kept the booze. I grabbed an unopened bottle of Maker's Mark bourbon and two dirty glasses.

When I returned to my room, Lola was naked and sweaty, and sitting at the head of the bed, holding a loaded Magnum. I knew it was loaded because I kept it that way in the drawer of my night-stand. She pointed the gun at me and thumbed back the hammer. I had to go anyway, so I pissed my pants. Only I wasn't wearing any. Instead, I soiled a perfectly good blanket hanging over the foot of the bed. Now, don't get me wrong; I've had plenty of intimidating guns aimed my way. But with a dame who enjoys a good dose of punishment with her sex behind the trigger—well, that's a whole other genre.

"Sorry 'bout this, Johnny," she said. "But they left me no choice."

I didn't have to ask who "they" were—the "they" who turned the woman I loved against me. I set the booze and glasses down and calmly collected myself.

"You should've just done the job, baby," she said.

"What do you know about it?"

"Nothing."

I was tired of hearing how no one knew anything about the job, yet found it fit to ask me why I didn't do it.

"So, what do the Lampleys have on you, doll?" I asked. "Or is it just the money?"

"They were gonna send pictures and video to my family."

"Pictures and video?"

"You know the type I mean, baby," she said, chewing her bottom lip.

"What do you care? You hate your family."

"Yes, I do. But then there is the money."

I knew it. There was always money. People were goddamn leeches when it came to a meaty payoff. Not that I was worth the price of the bullet.

"And I've wanted out of this life for a long time now," she added.

There seemed to be a lot of that going around.

"I told Carson to send the raunchy stuff, anyway. He enjoyed it well enough," she said, with pools of tears glistening in her eyes. "Maybe my father will too. Mommy really could use a good fuck-ing."

Tears rolled over her cheeks like high tide, and suddenly it was like an After School Special. The type where the angry teen runs away and finds her place in life as a sex toy, only to emerge at a pivotal point in her crappy little life where she needs and wants that parental comfort she once despised. Now, my beautiful Lola was broken down on my urine-soaked bed, swinging a gun, with the intention of putting a hole in me the size of a grapefruit. I'd call that pretty goddamn pivotal.

Foremost in my mind was walking out of that room alive. And with any hope, taking Lola with me.

"Listen, doll," I said, taking a step closer.

"Don't move, baby, or I'll have to plug you."

I stood like a statue, but had the distinct feeling her nerve to pull the trigger had faded.

"I can fix this," I said.

"They'll cut me up and feed me to the coyotes if I let you live."

"Trust me, I can fix it."

"Nobody can fix this. They're the Lampleys. You don't fix the Lampleys."

"You kill them," I broke in. "And it won't be milk baths and lol-lipops, but that is exactly what I'm gonna do."

"You would do that to save me?" she asked.

"And me," I said as I moved toward her and gently took the

cannon from her hands and unloaded it. "And if you really want to get out of this life ..."

A blinding flash of pain bit into my lower abdomen just inches from my left hipbone, followed by the chilling sensation of blood streaming down my leg and between my toes. I staggered back and slumped down into an old leather chair, clutching my wound.

Lola kept yelling and crying that she was sorry, and I kept cussing and groaning that I was pig-stuck.

My blood dripped from Lola's hand. She had stabbed me with, of all things, a sterling corkscrew, engraved with a queer little *L*.

Once the hysterics calmed, Lola came to my side with apologies and a piss-covered blanket to soak up some of the blood.

"We can get out of this," I said.

"How?"

"I know where we can get enough cash that the two of us could disappear forever."

"Where?" she asked.

"I don't know. Anyplace in the world you wanna go."

"No," she said. "Where can you get the money?"

***

I piled everything I would need—including the bottle of bourbon—into an old, primer-colored pickup I kept parked in front of room number twelve. I climbed into the heap with a grunt and a dish sponge pressed to my uncorked gut. I drove back to the Lampley Estate and parked twenty-five yards outside the gates.

I saw the gates open as I approached on foot. The banker's car pulled out, and Duke and Charlie—the other half of the security team—stepped out behind it.

Charlie spun at the sound of my footsteps, pulling his gun.

"Johnny, you frightened the shit out of me, man."

"Sorry, Charlie."

Charlie holstered his gun with a goofy grin.

Duke noticed my bloody pants. "You okay, Johnny?"

They weren't the reactions I was expecting, but good to see, nonetheless, because since they hadn't shot me, I presumed they knew nothing of The Lampleys' attempt on my life.

"Yeah, I'm dandy," I said. "Just a little tussled, that's all."

"You need a word with Mitch?" Charlie asked.

"No, not exactly." I stepped closer to them. "What I need, boys, is for you to turn your backs, let me walk into that house, and kill the Lampleys."

"Johnny ..."

I cut Duke off, and said, "I'll pay you each a hundred grand."

Duke and Charlie gave each other curious eyes. It was like feeding double-glazed donuts to potbellied cops.

"One-seventy-five apiece," Duke finally said.

"I'll tell you what," I said as I calmly took my .45 from my lower back and let it dangle at my side so they could get a real good look at it. "I'll pay you fifty thousand apiece and promise not to murder your families. How 'bout that?"

"Okay, Johnny," Duke said, averting his eyes from my gun as Charlie nervously stood by.

"And I want you two to take a drive out to Devil's Cobblestone ... you know the place?"

"Yeah, I know the place," Charlie said.

"There's a narrow gully that runs through it. I want you to push in a quarter mile west of the gully, and dig me some holes. I'll pay you off when I get there with the bodies and we'll all part ways. Understood?"

"Three holes?" Duke asked.

I took some time before I answered. "Yeah, three holes."

I watched Duke and Charlie drive out of the gates and then pulled my truck up to the gothic-styled mansion. I felt queasy as I broke the seal on the Maker's Mark and took more than a few belts. I took a deep breath, climbed out of the truck, and entered the mansion quietly, carefully, with a simple plan: quick and merciless.

I found Mitch first, in his office pouring himself the drink he never offered me, a Remy Martin. I slipped in and opened his carotid artery with a fancy scrimshawed letter opener from his desk. It happened so fast, he barely knew I was in the same room. I made sure he saw me as I watched the amazement on his face drain into a blood-sucking gurgle. When he was finally gone, I gladly washed the vindication down with the Remy.

In the hallway leading to Carson's bedroom, an awful smell hung in the air. An evil aroma that was so heavy, I felt it soaking into my pores. The microwaved asshole of a cadaver, maybe. Sharp pains were shooting through my legs and abdomen as I tried to spit out the smell's taste. I took shallow breaths, trying to avoid the stench as I readied my gun and crept into Carson's room.

There was no sign of Carson, and the smell was tenfold. Then I gathered enough commonsense to ease open the bathroom door. And there Carson sat, on the toilet, dropping a deuce, stewing in his own repugnant odor of what had to be a bowlful of deviled eggs and boiled cabbage. Downright sickening.

Carson looked up at me in genuine, speechless horror as I squeezed a round off into his left foot. Two toes shot off like scattering mice and I flinched like some sheepish dame. Carson was screaming and wailing, so I put another slug through the shinbone of his right leg and listened to him yell some more.

I had no speech prepared, but found myself speaking anyway. "You've taken everything from me but my life," I said.

Carson said a few vile things that might have passed for words, but I paid little attention. What I did do was shoot him in his left thigh. And I must have nicked the artery, because for a second it looked like he was ejaculating blood. When he looked down at the spurting wound, he proceeded to puke all over himself. That caused me to puke all over myself. When I did, I tasted the iron and salt of my own blood. Every time Carson spewed, I spewed. It was ridiculous. And Holy Christ, the smells.

We went through three or four rounds of upchucks before I finally shot Carson in the chest. As his lifeless body slowly slumped forward, I put a final bullet into the top of his skull. It popped like a pudding-filled piñata.

I puked again.

I never found Terry in the house, but I did find Mitch's money right where he had told me it was. Only there wasn't seven to eight hundred grand beneath the closet's floorboards like he guessed. There was closer to a million-seven.

***

I pulled up to the spot at Devil's Cobblestone and staggered out of the truck.

"Damn, you look like shit," Charlie said.

"As long as I don't smell like it."

Duke and Charlie had dug three of the most pristine graves I'd ever seen. And I'd seen and dug more than my fair share over the years. I paid the boys off with a hundred grand of Mitch Lampley's money and gave them a good luck farewell. Then I got to work.

The desert night was as cold and silent as Elvis. I was tired and weak and freezing and bleeding and pissed off. I buried Mitch and Carson Lampley in their holes and slapped their dirt lids down with a spoon-faced shovel as the glow of my truck's headlights spilled over my dusty boots.

Oh, yeah. And I needed a fucking cigarette.

Soon I was flooded with the glow of a second set of headlights. I turned around as Terry's Mercedes came to a jarring halt in a puff of dust and dirt. Terry popped out of the car like a jack in the box. He was covered in blood with torment and stress ripped across his face. He also had what looked a hell of a lot like a .38 revolver tucked in the front of his pants.

Duke and Charlie had known Terry wasn't in the house. And I never thought to ask. I figured it was Duke who called Terry and dropped the events of the evening. I wouldn't have expected anything less.

Terry and I stared at each other while the dirty, desert air settled in at our feet.

"Good to see you, Terry."

"I went by the house, Johnny," he said with a nervous hiccup in his tone.

"Yeah, I'm sorry about the mess."

"What the hell did you do?"

"I did you a favor," I said as I stepped aside offering Terry a good gander at the graves—two filled, one ready and waiting.

"And I'll probably appreciate it later," he said, resting his hand on the butt of his gun. "But where's the fucking money, Johnny?"

"What are your intentions here?" I asked, before coughing blood into my hand.

"What are yours?"

"Well, I intend to walk out of here if able. Just waiting on my second wind."

"I need that money."

"You just inherited a multibillion-dollar organization."

"I'm nothing like my brothers, Johnny. You know that better than anyone."

"Do I? Whose blood are you wearing?"

Terry paused then slowly looked down at his bloody clothes. When he looked back up, I could see anger dancing in the teary wet of his eyes.

"You should have just done the job. Why couldn't you have just done the job?"

"Because you were the fucking job!"

Terry's face went a sickish green, and I hoped like hell he didn't blow chunks, because I didn't have the energy left for that. "Why?" he whispered.

"Because they were assholes."

Terry understood what I was saying without me having to say it. He didn't fit their mold. I figured he deserved his individuality. I'll say it again; the job was wrong.

"Fuck 'em," he said, wiping away tears. "They got what they deserved."

"Whose blood is that, Terry?" I asked again. "What have you done tonight?"

"I want that money. And if you can't give it to me, I will kill her."

"Who?"

Terry tossed a bloody handkerchief to my feet. I winced in pain as I bent down to inspect it. I unwrapped the contents—a dame's pinky finger with dark nail polish.

"Lola," he said.

"Terry, you don't wanna do this."

"I'm buying a new life, no matter the cost."

I slowly rose to my feet. "That money is my way out, too. You know they'll come for me. I've gotta disappear, too."

Terry tossed another handkerchief. I held my bleeding abdomen and bent down to inspect it. I unwrapped the contents—a thumb. I presumed from the same hand.

"Now tell me where the money is."

"No," I said through gritted teeth as I managed to stand again.

"Goddamn it!" he yelled at the moon in frustration.

"This is gonna end badly for one of us."

"Maybe for both of us, Johnny."

"Nah, neither of us is that lucky."

Terry drew his .38 and fired a good quarter of a second before I squeezed the trigger of my .45. I felt hot lead whiz past my head as Terry's chest exploded in bloodied confetti. His body wilted to the ground.

I could hear Terry breathing through blood and bile as I stepped over to him and dropped to my knees to see if there was any chance of him surviving. There wasn't.

I wiped away a tear or two of my own, and held his hand until he was gone.

"I'll see you soon, my friend."

I crawled over to the truck and pulled myself up. I was weakening fast. Dizzy. My eyes where heavy and I wanted to sleep, but I still had work to do.

I dragged Terry to the third hole, which was never intended for him, and I gently slid him into it. Then I went back to the truck and told Lola that I loved her. I kept repeating it to her as I lifted her body out of the truck, carried her, and gently placed her into the hole with Terry. I positioned their bodies affectionately. Then I buried them.

Terry's brothers would have been impressed. The way he pressed me with that John Wayne swagger took balls. But not nearly the set it took for him to hack off the fingers of his lovely she-male and try to pass them off as my Lola's. Poor son of a bitch couldn't have known she was already dead.

Back at the motel, after I had told Lola about Mitch's hidden loot, she came at me again with the corkscrew. I didn't realize how hard I had twisted her head, until her neck snapped like a pretzel.

Funny how things play out.

I climbed into the truck and melted back into the seat next to the big bag of blood money and the bottle of bourbon. I'd been slowly bleeding to death for close to five hours now. My face looked back at me from the mirror with sunken eyes and skin the texture and shade of custard.

The sun was rising over the horizon in layers of lavender when I heard the door of Terry's Mercedes open and close. I heard footsteps drag over the scorched earth until the face of a dame, the angelic face of an eight-fingered Carnival, appeared like a mirage in the passenger side window. Carnival's left hand was wrapped in bloodied gauze and hanging over the edge of the door. She was as calm and cool as a cucumber. And I'll be damned if there wasn't a freshly lit cigarette perched between her gorgeous, glossy lips. I managed to will my hand to move. I gently plucked the cigarette from her mouth and tucked it into my own. Her lipstick tasted like sweet, juicy apples.

Carnival gave me an amorous smile and slowly eased the bag of money out of the truck. Then she disappeared.

So, now here I am, sitting with a lapful of blood, sucking on one of the best goddamn one-point-seven-million-dollar cigarettes I've ever tasted, and I'm laughing.

And laughing.

Funny how things play out.

Contemporary Press **current titles**

Small Brutal Incidents
by Michael Dittman

When Stephen Ketchum, the son of a prominent mill owner, is found murdered, the family takes matters into their own hands, seeking the type of justice the law can't provide. Home from a brutal stint in the Pacific, WWII veteran Graeme Burns's life changes forever when the Ketchum family forces him to find their murderer.

ISBN 0976657929

Digging the Vein
by Tony O'Neill

Tony O'Neill's astonishing debut is based on his own experiences as an addict and sideman to acts as diverse as the Brian Jonestown Massacre, Kenickie, and Marc Almond. Through the eyes of his anonymous narrator, see what few tourists ever will: the needle exchanges, methadone clinics, short-let motels, and scoring spots beneath the wings of the City Of Angels.

ISBN 0976657910

The Bride of Trash
by Mike Segretto

Good ol' boy Wizzer Whale has fallen deeply in love with a blood-thirsty monster, and now, the newlyweds are running for their lives. Their romance is a raucous and warped homage to the lurid, gory, ultra-campy, B-monster movies of the 1950s. Seeping with bad taste, you'll stay awake, gasping and guffawing long past midnight!

ISBN 0976657902

I, An Actress: The Autobiography of Karen Jamey
as told to Jeffrey Dinsmore
When little Karen Hitler's mother runs off to become
a hobo, she and her father change their names and
move to Los Angeles. Dark, slapstick comedy and
merciless Hollywood clichés rule this hilarious story
of Karen's manic rise to the silver screen—and her
tragic (and largely ignored) fall.
ISBN 0974461490

Danger City
edited by Jess Dukes, Jeffrey Dinsmore,
and Mike Segretto
The thirteen stories in this collection showcase some
of the finest contemporary pulp from across the land.
Bleak tales of payoffs gone wrong, crooked cops,
stone-hearted women, and the undead inhabit these
pages. Once you begin wandering it's shadowy alley-
ways, you may find it impossible to leave.
ISBN 0974461482

Dead Rite
by Jim Gilmore
When an unpopular video game mogul is discovered
in a shallow grave, Officer Hicks does things by the
book—until the trail of clues leads straight back to
him! Fast-paced and deadly, this is one man's dark trip
through the riches of sunny Hollywood.
ISBN 0974461474

How to Smash Everyone to Pieces
by Mike Segretto

Flanked with a lethal but supportive crew of misfits, ex-stunt woman and champion wisecracker Mary sets off on a homicidal, cross-country campaign to free the love of her life from the clutches of the law.

ISBN 0974461466

G.O.P. D.O.A.
by Jay Brida

While the city braces for 20,000 Republicans to descend on New York, a Brooklyn political operative named Flanagan uncovers a bizarre plot that could trigger a red, white, black, and blue nightmare.

ISBN 0974461458

Johnny Astronaut
by Rory Carmichael (a/k/a Jeffrey Dinsmore)

In the future, disco is king. Johnny is a hard-boiled, hard-drinking P.I. who is caught between a vindictive ex-wife, a powerful crime boss, and a mysterious book that changes his life forever.

ISBN 0974461431

Down Girl
by Jess Dukes

In *Down Girl*, a low-rent escort struggles for every cent she ever made until she meets Anton, willing to give her more cash than she's ever imagined ... for one small favor.

ISBN 0974461415

Dead Dog
by Mike Segretto

A curmudgeonly shut-in's life is turned inside out when he becomes involved with a trash-talking femme fatale and a dog that won't shut up. *Dead Dog* is a riotous road trip from an Arizona trailer park to hell.

ISBN 0974461407

contemporary press

Contemporary Press (est. 2003) is committed to truth, justice, and going our own way. When Big Publishing dies, we're the cockroaches who will devour their bones and dance on their graves.